WAKING UP

An Anesthetist's Diary

MARY ELLEN SPRUELL

PAGE PUBLISHING, INC.
New York, NY

First originally published by Page Publishing, Inc. 2018

ISBN 978-1-64138-690-6 (Paperback)
ISBN 978-1-64138-691-3 (Digital)

Printed in the United States of America

CONTENTS

Introduction...5

1. Doctor Sing...7

2. Changes 14

3. The Aorta...21

4. Blind Date 25

5. New Boss 27

6. Dancing 30

7. Apron Removal 32

8. Bust Development......................................35

9. Impure Thoughts......................................37

10. How We Met 45

11. Power Play..57

12. Promotion..61

13. The Students 66

14. The Gentle Man.......................................72

15. The Ashram...78

16. Two Patients..84

17. Karma..87

18. A Mistake..92

19. The Letter..96

20. Another Closet..101

21. The Tooth...105

22. The Tumor..107

23. Emergency...110

24. Merging...113

25. Big Blue...122

26. Click..124

27. The Vision..127

28. The Rose...129

29. The Power..133

30. A Miracle...136

31. Let Me Call You Sweetheart...........................140

32. Forgiveness in 1984....................................143

33. The Fast Lane..145

Afterword...147

INTRODUCTION

WAKING UP IS a novel inspired by true events. Some diary entries are total fabrications. Some characters are a compilation of people I knew. This work is dedicated to the present, past, and future practitioners of the fine tradition of nurse anesthesia, the CRNAs. I also want to acknowledge all the talented, caring anesthesiologists and wonderful surgeons with whom I have worked day and night, behind those operating-room doors. I especially want to thank the two brothers and their partners, who treated us CRNAs as equals, who encouraged us to keep learning and expanding our expertise, who made sure we had a 401k plan.

The field of anesthesia in the 1970s and '80s was a bit more primitive. What is described here could have happened in a surgical suite anywhere in the world during those years.

The spiritual experiences revealed here are archetypical and not wedded to any particular religious organization. No spiritual tradition had any direct input into the writing of this work.

A special thanks to my devoted husband, Lee, for his hours of reading and critiquing many revisions. And I greatly appreciate all of you other wonderful sweethearts whom I shall not name. Thank you for reading, editing, and encouraging me to bring this story to life.

DOCTOR SING

October 1976

MY BODY DRAPES flaccidly across the stiff plastic-coated mattress as I float in an ocean of nothingness. I breathe in and out gently. There is a slight hint of antiseptic wafting into the dark room from under the door. Far off, a telephone jangles louder and louder—insidious and insistent, pushing me from the void. I wake up. My arm pokes out of the covers and gropes for the receiver.

"Anesthesia," I murmur quickly.

The hospital operator yells, "Code 99! Accident Ward!"

"On my way!" I slam down the phone, jam bare feet into clogs, dash out the door, up the hallway, and *clack-clack-clack* down the dank stairwell.

I'm waved forward into the cubicle by a couple of bleary-eyed nurses. Squinting under glaring lights I take in the scene. The big clock on the tile wall shows 3:10 a.m.

"He just came in. Cardiac arrest!" the sweating doctor barks at me as he rhythmically presses on the man's chest. Nearby some inane music sets the beat.

"It's Dr. Sing, Chief of Anesthesia!" he says, voice cracking.

My jaw drops with an involuntary gasp.

No! It can't be! My boss!

I feel my throat close involuntarily to prevent acid from rising further. Shivers contract my shoulders in spite of the sweltering room.

I'm at the head of the stretcher now, laryngoscope and tube in hand. Everyone stands still as I open the middle-aged Asian man's blue-gray mouth, insert the metal instrument, and slide the endotracheal tube down his throat. The bag is hooked up, and I squeeze life-giving oxygen into his severely deprived system.

The nurse takes a turn with the chest compressions. Her cologne mingles with the salty scent of fresh sweat as her hands bounce up and down on the man's barrel chest. The ominous silence from the heart monitor amplifies her grunting exertion. There is a soft snap of a rib cracking.

Fluids and drugs are given. Everything we know to do is done, but the man's heart will never beat again. It has worked all it can, and it is finished. At 3:45 a.m. it is over.

I can't believe it. This is such a good man. My hand rests against his round face. How cool his cheek is already. Lying there covered with a sheet, surrounded by the now-futile equipment, he seems as serene and inscrutable in death as he was in life. Hot tears blur my vision. The searing shaft of loss pushes deep. I feel my face flush as I strain to contain the shock and grief.

In the distance, as if on cue, the radio plays the Kansas song "Dust in the Wind": "Dust in the wind. All we are is dust in the wind." My tears blind me.

Dr. Greenberg, the backup anesthesiologist bursts into the room, his sparse gray hair flying in all directions. The doctor on the scene briefs him. For a long time, he stands with his arm around my shoulders.

"What can I say? I got here as quickly as humanly possible."

I shake my head sadly. "We did our best. We couldn't bring him back."

The rest of that night I lie curled in the fetal position in the call-room bed, deeply nested under the blankets, wet eyes open wide.

The dark room, indeed the entire hospital, seems uncommonly quiet now.

Every emotion takes its turn as I remember so many things about my former mentor. Dr. Sing was a very droll teacher. I never saw him get angry. His teaching method was much more subtle. He wanted his students to always remain totally focused, in the true sense of the "watcher," as anesthetists are known. We were taught to sweep our eyes across the dials on the anesthesia machine, intravenous fluids, the patient, and the room every thirty seconds to detect any changes. When I was a first-year student, I experienced firsthand his creative way of driving this lesson home. I never forgot it.

I was giving anesthesia to a young man with an inguinal hernia in OR 2. He was already asleep. I had a black latex mask strapped to his face. A little plastic airway was between his teeth, and I was squeezing the anesthesia bag to assist his steady breathing. The machine pumped a mixture of oxygen, nitrous oxide, and some halothane into the bag. The patient's blood pressure registered just right; his heart was beating nice and slow.

I was nervous all the time as a student, but when everything was going smoothly like this, I could ever so slightly relax.

The surgeon stood with his scalpel in hand and asked me, "All right to start?" Dr. Sing liked to assign the newer anesthesia students with this doctor because he didn't holler at us if the patient moved a little when he made the first cut. We could be, shall we say, less than perfect.

"Yes, sir," I said in a strong voice that disguised my insecurity. I was pretty sure the patient wouldn't move.

With a quick swipe of the surgeon's wrist, the small steel blade flicked across the orange-painted square of exposed groin, followed instantly by a thin red line that glistened under the lights and spread until its trickle was blotted up by the scrub nurse. My patient didn't move a muscle. I could breathe a little now. So far so good.

The door behind us opened. Dr. Sing came in and stood there nonchalantly watching. He must have been observing me through the window to see if this kid was going to move. I was positive of it.

The surgeon worked methodically with the small pile of innards, which made no sense at all to me at the time. I was sure glad he knew what all that stuff was.

Gradually I noticed my patient's pulse racing faster and his blood pressure rose higher and higher. What's going on here? I saw sweat breaking out on the young man's forehead. This can't be good! Frantically I checked my lines. My IV was okay, but the guy's heartbeat was up to 120 now! Oh my gosh! Was that the patient's hand rising up toward the surgeon's rear end? How could this be?

I jerked around and saw the gauges on my machine—no anesthesia! Dr. Sing had turned off everything except for the oxygen. He stood there stone-faced, arms crossed. I grabbed the sodium Pentothal for a quick fix. Wilma, the circulating nurse, quietly leaned on the patient's now-awakened hand to prevent it from grabbing Dr. Sefford's bottom. For a forty-five-second eternity, Wilma and the young man's hand arm-wrestled while the drug traveled from the IV site, up the vein of his arm, through his heart, and into his brain. Slowly the recalcitrant limb relaxed. Wilma secured it gently on the arm board. I could tell from the woman's bent head that behind her mask, Wilma had a big smirk. I turned the anesthesia back on and looked around. Dr. Sing and I shared a long look. He had a smirk behind his mask too.

"I guess it was a little longer than thirty seconds since I checked that machine, huh?" I whispered.

"I guess so." He stalked out of the room.

I settle deeper under the covers now, the plastic mattress creaking under me. We didn't ask that young man if he remembered anything. Dr. Sing never looked for trouble.

Even though diethyl ether was generally no longer in use in the1970s, the good doctor wanted to be sure his anesthesia students had a complete training. He wanted us to be prepared to work anywhere, even under primitive conditions. Therefore, he insisted that I administer open-drop ether to two children who needed to have their tonsils out. This was a whole new ball game. First of all, ether is a very volatile, flammable, and explosive liquid, especially in the presence of oxygen. To prevent the possibility of sparking an explosion, oxygen and electric cautery couldn't be used. Rubber mats were placed on the floor, and we couldn't wear anything synthetic, not even underwear. For years operating rooms had been designed with all electrical outlets installed about five feet up the walls, since heavier than air, ether vapor settles low to the floor and can travel considerable distances toward an ignition source.

It takes fifteen or twenty minutes before a surgical level of anesthesia is reached. There is a masklike frame covered with seventeen layers of gauze covering the patient's face. We then drip the ether liquid from about six inches high onto this mask for twenty minutes. Of course everyone there is also breathing the stuff. It's very pungent.

One ether characteristic is a long lag time after respiratory arrest to when cardiac arrest occurs. So the trick with tonsillectomy anesthesia is to have the child breathe the ether until he stops breathing. The mask is then removed and the surgeon yanks out a tonsil. This stimulus gets the kid breathing again. So you put the ether mask back on his face and drip some more of the awful stuff until respiratory arrest occurs again. The second tonsil is yanked out and the procedure is finished.

That experience I will never forget. Luckily both children survived, but I don't ever want to do that again. No airway protection, no oxygen, and an explosion threat? Please. With Dr. Sing gone, ether will likely never be used at Robertsboro Hospital again.

As the first gray light of dawn slips in the call room window, I remember the way Dr. Sing avoided talking of his background. I learned that he had been a surgeon in his homeland of China. When he immigrated here and found he would have to go back to medical school, he decided to study anesthesia instead.

Once while getting a young fellow ready the patient asked him, "Where did you go to school, Dr. Sing?"

"Oh, I didn't go school. I from Chinese laundry next door," the doctor quipped in his heavy accent, making it seem true. Then he pushed in the Pentothal and that was the end of the conversation.

What kind of nightmare might that induce in this patient? I can only imagine. But I had to laugh at the doctor's audacity.

I shift in bed and think of another time. I had just anesthetized a man who was having some teeth extracted. Dr. Sing stood by to help me with the nasal intubation. The patient's breath smelled strong, like something dead and rotten. The stench made my eyes water. "He sure has bad breath," I commented.

Dr. Sing retorted, "Bad breath better than no breath at all!" And he laughed.

He laughed so well. Oh, how I will miss that laugh! The thought gets me weeping again. I overflow with tears and gratitude. That good little man in Accident Ward awaiting the mortician offered me great comfort in the past. He gave me the opportunity to attend his school for nurse anesthetists and changed the course of my life and those of my three children.

Blotting my eyes on the sheet, I picture them at home, Andrew, Amanda and Lydia. Soon Miss Ellis will be rousting them out of their beds and cooking breakfast while they get ready for school. They are great kids. Thirteen-year-old Andrew thinks he's pretty grown up now, and so does Amanda, for that matter. She will be eleven in July and is already Miss Fashion Model. And Lydia has a mind of her own, even though she's only nine.

Miss Ellis is another great blessing in our lives. After my husband Paul and I split up, I needed to see how I could support the children. I was desperate to keep us together in the tiny Cape Cod house that we bought a decade earlier with four hundred dollars down payment.

I had big decisions to make on my own after he moved out. First, I got a full time job at Robertsboro Hospital in the pulmonary function lab. Then I put an ad in the paper for a nanny who would work for room and board. We got Miss Ellis, quite an elegant woman who admitted to being in her sixties. But I suspect she was using a lady's prerogative. Miss Ellis had been a housemother at a private girls' school until she broke her ankle and decided to retire. We trusted each other right away.

Discovering that Miss Ellis would also cook was delightful. She never invited me to call her by her first name, but we certainly have become a great team. We mostly agree, and I help with her medical problems. She advises me on clothes and, more importantly, men. With Miss Ellis in charge at home, I can concentrate on my anesthesia work.

I sit up and check my watch. What a relief. No emergency calls for the last three hours. After my twenty-four hour shift I half-heartedly brush my hair, throw on an overcoat and head out the door. I feel drained and listless. Dr. Greenberg will have to deal with the rest of our staff. I can't face my coworkers yet to discuss the horror of losing our beloved chief.

CHAGES

AS I DRAW the cloudy fall morning into my lungs, the taste of burnt leaves taints the air. I need to be more exhausted if I expect to get any sleep today. Good thing Michelle is meeting me at the gym. Already I'm compartmentalizing my grief. Foreseeing my best friend's reaction to the news of Dr. Sing's failed resuscitation, a sick gallows smile creeps across my face.

Michelle had been instrumental in my decision to apply for anesthesia training. She was a good "shrink" during my bad times with Paul. I'll always be indebted for her insightful listening and good opinions, which she doesn't mind dishing out as needed. Seems she never tires of my drama. Her Larry is nice but a little boring. Could that be why she enjoys all my stuff? There's no actual suffering involved on her part. I don't care. Good ole Michelle helped me weather it.

The aerobics class is already in full swing. Michelle's willowy features stand out above the other jiggling ladies. She grins at me and waves in time with the pulsing drumbeat from the instructor's tape player. By the time I change, some of the women's leotards are already stained with perspiration. I'm good and late.

It feels therapeutic for my weary body to leap and twist, turning and bending to the high piercing commands of Tina, who goads us on.

"Keep going, ladies! Rock it! Rock it! 5-6-7-8! Rock it! Rock it! Do it! Do it! 9-10-11-12!" Our sneakers pound the cement floor in unison. I put the dreadfulness out of my mind and focus on the dance routine. After Tina finishes with us, Michelle and I lift weights. Lying on my back, a five-pound weight swinging up and down in each hand, I mentally repeat my usual affirmation, Bigger Bust! Bigger Bust! Bigger Bust! I'm almost as tall as Michelle but thinner on top. I believe that somehow my mind will influence this flat-chested body. At least I'm giving it a good try with the barbells. Bigger Bust! Bigger Bust! Bigger Bust! There. That's enough o' that! Finally we leave and head for the coffee shop where Michelle hears about my shocking night on call. As always, I get her full attention. Afterward I feel more peaceful and head for home.

The dark day makes the house less welcoming. Miss Ellis will be out with friends until evening and the children are at school. Blanketed in loneliness, I slump on the couch with some hot tea laced with a tiny bit of Miss Ellis's cooking sherry. Dr. Sing's sudden death is affecting me in a way I didn't expect. I remember the nightmare for the first time in years. I jump up and grab the cookie jar and carefully place it in front of me on the old glass-topped coffee table.

Nibbling on a chocolate chip cookie, I relive when I was first married to Paul. We were so in love, even after our little Andrew was born. During those early years, I had a recurring bad dream. In it, my husband was dead. It felt so real I'd wake up in a cold sweat, picturing every detail of his funeral. That dream plagued me for a long time.

After little Amanda was born, we were forced to move out of our little second floor apartment. The owner of the old house, an elderly gentleman who lived downstairs was always cold, so he would stoke the old coal burning furnace until the water in our radiators was boiling. It was so hot we kept the windows open all winter.

Afraid the kids could be burned, we moved in with my widowed Aunt Olive temporarily. She collected knickknacks so I had fun keeping two toddlers from her intricate treasures which were displayed everywhere. A nonsmoker, she collected interesting ashtrays which were strategically placed for her guests. My favorite depicted Jesus on the cross. When the cigarette butt was extinguished, Jesus took the hit.

Aunt Olive loved attending Irish wakes, about three or four evenings a week, whether or not she knew the deceased person. She called herself "the merry widow." It was navy bean and ham soup on Saturday, with her seven 'n' seven waiting on the kitchen counter. Her hard and fast rule was no alcohol till 11 a.m. And she stuck to it religiously.

She and her girlfriends partied on Saturday nights, and with our bedroom right next to the bathroom, I often awakened to the sound of an extremely full bladder being emptied for several long minutes. Apparently using the bar's restroom was not considered "lady-like."

Religious in the true sense, she pranced right down the center aisle during Sunday Mass still wearing her Saturday night finery and a fantastic hat.

In the meantime, thanks to lack of privacy and my careful practice of the rhythm method of birth control, Paul and I had limited intimacy. He got more and more frustrated and irritable with the whole situation. Finally, after much soul searching, I turned against my religion. I began to take the revolutionary new Pill which had just come on the market. The first month on the drug my digestive system caused so much discomfort I stopped and went back to the old rhythm birth control. Paul was nervous. "Are you sure it's safe for us now?" he asked. I reassured him. "I figured it out and I'm sure it's all right." Nine months later we had our third child, Lydia. Being childless herself, Aunt Olive was thrilled that a child had been conceived in her home. She delightedly became little Lydia's godmother.

When we got a mortgage we moved into this little house. After that there were too many difficulties and disappointments. Paul couldn't keep a job. One Saturday the gas company meter reader came by. I mentioned that those meter readers didn't usually work on Saturday. His face dropped. He ran into the bedroom, rifled through his desk and found the disconnection notice dated that Saturday.

My horrific temper affected the situation more than I like to admit. We were already sliding down a slippery slope when something worse happened. I hate the memory of that fateful October day five years ago as it flashes vividly in my mind.

The sun was streaming in onto the warm pile of clean laundry as I sat there lining up socks of various sizes and colors. Amanda tiptoed in and quickly closed the door. Methodically she moved the socks aside and climbed up on the bed, her round little face haloed in a froth of blond curls. She was grinning secretively and began to chatter about yesterday's trip to the park with Daddy. Even though Paul had a hard time keeping a job, he was great with the kids on Sundays and evenings when I was working at the local hospital. My hospital paycheck was the only way we could make the mortgage payment.

"Another girl came to the park with us," Amanda started.

"Oh, did you take a girlfriend with you?"

"No, it was a big girl. She had pretty yellow hair. She's Daddy's friend."

The blood thumped against my eardrums, and my arms went weak from the weight of the tee shirt I was folding.

"They were sittin' together on the quilt while Andy and me and Lydia rode the swings 'n' stuff. And they were smokin' a stinky little cigarette. Yuck!"

I mentally screamed. Paul doesn't smoke! They must have smoked pot! This can't be happening!

Paul had been sweeter those last three months. I never suspected it would be our last summer together. In July, Mom and I had taken the kids to the beach for a week. As Paul temporarily had a job, he joined us on the weekend. He'd just bought himself a motorcycle and rode it to the shore. We had a relaxing family day in the sun and the waves. That evening while Mom babysat, the two of us took off on the bike. Things felt different. His quietly sullen vibe was gone and Paul seemed more like a fun date than a resentful husband. Wearing a new pink blouse and a pair of snug-fitting dungarees, I sat close behind him, straddling the huge bike carefully. When Paul revved the motor, my arms went into a strangle grip around his thin waist with my breasts pressing up against him. I could feel the sunburn heat of his muscular back through his cheap tee shirt. Friction from the raucous vibrating charger tingled my nipples and deep parts. We careened through the darkness, all wind and roar and the smell of the sea and we laughed and laughed for the pure joy of it. The final bliss of a dying relationship.

Three months later, sitting with my daughter on our bed in the thin sun of a cold October day, I had wondered if that change in Paul had something to do with this yellow-haired person. Life had not been good for our years together. Paul never seemed happy. In fact he seemed to love suffering. Somehow a crisis with the car would always occur on the coldest night of the year and he'd have to work on it. We didn't have a garage so every hour or so, lean and mean Paul would lurch through the back door and hunch himself over a lit burner on the gas stove, straightening and flexing his greasy fingers over the flame.

Paul was one sexy dude and brilliant, but he sure could aggravate me. When I had to be on duty at the hospital, he'd come home late, and what a horrible battle that caused! I couldn't leave the kids home alone, but the day nurse couldn't leave her patients until I showed up. When he would finally pull into the driveway I'd start screaming and ranting at him and criticizing him every way I could think of. Sometimes he'd slap me to shut me up. Then I'd go to work.

I squirm on the couch, my shoulders round and arms embracing the big cold cookie jar. It's almost empty. I review for the hundredth time what turned out to be the final blow to a relationship I believed would last forever, or at least until my "death" nightmare came true.

"Who was the blond haired woman?" I asked.

Paul said, "Becky is her name and she's just a friend. No, there isn't anything physical between us; we're just intellectually stimulating for one another. Yes, you can meet her Friday evening."

When Becky arrived she looked good, with long, blond hair. And she was tall like me. I acted calm and friendly but my face felt hot and tight. I was acutely aware of intense energy in the living room as the three of us sat and chatted. The physical magnetism sparking between Paul and Becky in spite of the casual conversation completely locked me out. No matter what I heard, saw or wanted to believe, my guts knew. I had a big problem.

How do you survive total devastation of your world? You develop your repertoire. I hardened, and then softened. I pleaded. I explored the possibility of polygamy. I played the suicide role. We sought marriage counseling. He went to them. But after the counselors and the therapists talked to Paul privately they changed their approach. Whatever he told them, they understood that reconciliation was not an option. Finally Paul moved out. By then I felt relieved and drained.

Alone one bone-chilling Saturday night three months after he'd gone, I sat on the side of our bed. Wine had no effect. Valium couldn't take the pain away either. I was alone.

It was mind stopping, this aloneness.

I still remember vividly how I felt that evening:

I was sitting on the bed that celebrated so much fire, so many erotic moments.

Now it was very empty and very cold.

I was still.

All the nightmares I used to have about his death never prepared me for this.

I was totally unloved, maybe even unlovable.

I felt nothing.

Just alone.

Still.

I fell deep inside to the deepest place.

This is it.

I am nothing.

But I am.

I am alone and I'm okay.
Yes.
It's true.
Deep calm settles over me.
I experience the Truth.
I am nothing.
I am OK.
I am My Self.
I Am.
And the old heater in the hall closet kicked on with its usual loud droning *OOOOOMMMMMMMMMMMMM.*

My eyelids flutter, and I breathe deeply. The sun has come out, slanting through the living room window, making the small room cheerful and fresh. I stretch slowly and rousing, I glance over at the clock. Three o'clock. What a good sleep I had! I clear away the sherry bottle, cookie jar and my teacup. My sweet little family will be home soon.

THE AORTA

SOMETHING IS VERY wrong. Dolores Parker is never sick. But this morning she wakes to pain, deep, wrenching pressure in her gut. Through her thin nightgown, she can feel that her whole torso is hard and swollen and hot. It's hard to tell what part of her belly is the problem. When she tries to get out of bed she is knocked back by a flash of agony. Her breath catches in a high gasp. Even lying perfectly motionless, it hurts to breathe. Shallow, quick breaths jerk past her pale lips.

Weakly, "Help me, Jim! Help me." Her husband of forty-five years stirs, then sits up in bed. He sees her chalky face and grabs the phone. "Operator, we need an ambulance! Come quick!"

In the accident ward the lanky physician knows what is wrong even though he's a first-year resident. When he cautiously places his long fingers on the woman's abdomen it pulses like a time bomb. He can almost hear the thumping.

"Ruptured triple A!" he shouts to the nurse. "Type 'n' cross 'er 'n' get Shillinger in here!"

The pumping heart ejects blood into a great tree-trunk of an artery that carries it throughout the body. It is the aorta. This inch and a half thick pipe stretches from the chest down through the belly. It is elastic connective tissue which provides the strength needed to withstand the pressure produced by the heart's contractions. Unfortunately, cholesterol plaques have calcified and hardened Dolores's aorta. Over time, her pounding high blood pressure created a weak spot called an aneurysm. This weakened area slowly widened, becoming thinner and thinner. This morning that awful bubble burst. Even with prompt emergency surgery the rupture of an aortic aneurysm is often fatal. At this moment, Dolores' blood is being pumped under high pressure into her abdominal cavity.

I'm sitting on the vinyl couch in the OR lounge drinking hot coffee. My hand dangles a half-eaten chocolate doughnut above the cup. I'm totally focused on the dunking process, deftly jamming the soggy doughnut into my mouth before any falls into the cup or my lap. OR 1 nurses Wilma and Marie are there reading the newspaper, with the box of doughnuts between them. The intercom blasts. "Triple A in OR 1! STAT! Patient's on her way up. Dr. Shillinger's changing in the locker room."

Adrenalin rush triggers us into instant motion. Cheeks bulging with doughnut I glance at the clock. "10:30 a.m. At least it's not 10:30 p.m. Let's rock and roll! Get her blood up from the lab, will you, Wilma?"

Petite dark-haired Dr. Navana Micha is the anesthesiologist who follows me into the operating room. We quickly set up the drugs and equipment needed.

Wide-eyed and ashen-faced, Dolores Parker is wheeled into the OR. Like jungle vines, oxygen and intravenous lines, catheters and other tubes flow into her body. I take her hand. It is limp and cold. I look into her terrified eyes.

"We're going to take good care of you, Mrs. Parker."

Her pulse is weak and thready and blood pressure is borderline. We need to be careful to not stress her blood-starved heart any more than necessary during the induction of anesthesia.

After she is asleep, blustery Dr. Shillinger comes in, all business. IV fluids and blood are pouring into her arms at top speed when he makes the long incision on Dolores' abdomen. Hot fluid bubbles out of the widening crevice, then gushes in a crimson waterfall over the sterile drapes and down the sides of the OR table. It spreads unnoticed over the shoes of the team and forms a dark sticky puddle on the floor around their feet. The cut is extended from just below her breasts to her pubic area with a little semicircle diversion around her bellybutton. The surgeon's big meaty hands and arms plunge deep into the belly of clotting blood and intestines. He quickly grabs the still pulsing aorta just above the tear. With a grunt he clamps it. Suddenly the bleeding is under control. Simultaneously, the team breathes deeper as we move into the more routine part of the vascular repair.

Wiry-haired Dr. Earl Mitchell serves as surgical assistant. As the two men work they discuss how best to proceed. An artificial Dacron artery will be grafted to replace the ripped segment of Dolores Parker's aorta. They move with alacrity. Now that the aorta is clamped, her kidneys, bowels and legs are being deprived of circulation until the Dacron piece is sewn in.

At 1:15 pm, while Navana is out for a break, Dr. Shillinger looks toward the head of the table and tersely warns me.

"I'm taking off the clamp. You ready, Emily?" Since the graft is porous, blood always flows out through it when the clamp is removed and the aorta is opened up. It is designed that way. Dolores's natural clotting factors will seal off the pinholes in a minute or two and the inner surface will be like a natural blood vessel.

"IVs are wide open, Doctor. We're ready." I always love this part. It's weird to see all that red stuff spurting out of the sides of the new aorta and then suddenly stop. All eyes focus on the repaired vessel. The abdominal cavity quickly fills up with rich, viscous liquid. But it doesn't slow down. Again blood overflows across the drapes and cascades down in little rivulets, falling on the sopping sheets around the doctors' dark-stained shoes. Behind my mask, I deeply inhale the metallic fresh-blood smell that permeates the room. This is a bad one.

Grudgingly, Dr. Shillinger reclamps the hemorrhaging aorta. I announce, "She's had six units so far. We're ordering more." Wilma phones the blood bank. Navana quietly enters the OR. Eyebrows up, she silently communicates her question to me. I frown and slightly shake my head. The bleed has not been stopped.

"Take a break, Em. I'll keep pumping the blood in."

At 4:00 p.m. and again at six-thirty the vessel is briefly opened, then reclamped. Something is still bleeding. Twelve, then fifteen units of blood and other stabilizing fluids are administered. Every time we think we're caught up there is another blood bath. Our hands, arms and scrub dresses are splattered. The dials on the anesthesia machine are tacky and smeared. The physical exertion of keeping Dolores Parker alive is taking its toll. My arms ache from squeezing the blood pumps for so many hours. I've never seen Dr. Shillinger struggling like this. The usual banter between him and Earl faded hours ago. Now Shillinger snaps, "No, Earl! Not that!" Then Earl retorts defensively and a brief argument ensues. But mostly the two surgeons work in silence. Anxiety hangs over them like a guillotine. Only the rhythmic hiss of the ventilator and the intermittent suctioning of Dolores Parker's blood give voice to our fear and hope.

"We've got to keep going, Navana. We can't slow down now! We've got to keep her alive a little longer." We two anesthetists are totally exhausted. Finally, eleven hours and twenty-three pints of blood later, the surgery is finished. Dolores Parker is still alive. She has good circulation in both legs; all her vital signs are stable. Unfortunately, her kidneys are not working. She will need to go on dialysis.

A few weeks later Dr. Shillinger stops me in the hallway. "Dolores Parker is doing great! Even her kidneys have started working again. How 'bout that!"

"That's great news, Doctor!" The two of us grin at each other like little kids, remembering how we saved her life that bloody day.

24

BLIND 4 DATE

"THANKS, GINNY, I'LL see you tomorrow at six!" I hang up the phone and smile. Well, how amazing is that! I have a date with a marine! Isn't that nice! Ginny and Chuck planned a dinner for all of us to get together. John Somethin' or other. Good-lookin' too, she said. Who knows. I guess I'll find out at their house tomorrow.

I haven't felt like dating since Paul moved out, but I trust my neighbors down the street. We all went to parties together when Paul and I had been a couple. I'm pleased that they want their friend John to meet me. I feel honored and hope I don't disappoint them.

The next evening when Ginny opens the door, her eyes and smile go wide. I look darn good. My auburn hair is all curls around my face and I'm wearing a red angora sweater that had been a present from good ol' Paul a few years back. I'd love to see the look on his face if he could see me now! I smirk, wiggling my rear end a little in the snug black skirt. Ginny, bulging here and there in her short flowered dress, gives me a big hug.

"Come on in, sweetie! I want you to meet John Reikert. John, Emily."

The tall dark haired man briefly takes my hand, just long enough for me to feel his strength and nervousness. His palm is sweaty. My own feels like a cold fish, but John doesn't seem to mind. His eyes feast on me as we sit and chat. Now I begin to relax. He's just as uncomfortable with this blind date thing as I am.

Chuck, festive in his perennial Hawaiian shirt, hustles his burly frame around the room, serving beer and wine. He and Ginny are in high spirits, delighted with their matchmaking scheme. The four of us enjoy a lively discussion as we dive into Ginny's famous pasta primavera and garlic bread. No kissin' after this meal for sure. He's cute, but I'm in no hurry for that stuff anyway.

The evening wears on and when I say I have to get up early for work, John offers to walk me home. The sunny warmth of the day is gone now. When he notices my shivering he drapes his jacket around my shoulders. The sharp night air accentuates the smell of a man radiating from the warm garment. It envelops me. I breathe in long to get all the good out of it, like fresh-baked bread, as we stroll. His hand at my elbow, he asks me to go out dancing Saturday. My heart melts.

"Dancing! Oh I'd love it!"

At my door he maneuvers in for a kiss, but his seeking lips fall on the cool cheek I offer instead. He grins and retrieves his coat. "Saturday, then. I'll pick you up at eight." As I close the door behind me I breathe a big garlicky Wow! Dancing! Imagine. A man who likes to dance! I kick off my shoes and spin round and round the dim room, one, two, three; one two, three, humming a waltz, round and round!

NEW BOSS

AFTER THE SUDDEN death of Dr. Sing, our anesthesia department undergoes a difficult reorganization. By default, the position of Anesthesia Chief falls to Dr. Panute. He's in his forties and single. There are rumors of his womanizing escapades, but he obviously is not attracted to me.

I gotta try to keep my mouth shut. In the past, Panute and I often disagreed. Sometimes we'd argue about the actions of certain anesthesia drugs. He doesn't seem to study pharmacology texts in depth, and basically relies on what the drug sales reps tell him. Nurse anesthetists must pass an arduous certification exam plus earn twenty credits each year to maintain our credentials. To practice anesthesia doctors need an MD or DO license. Although the majority of physician anesthesiologists have also passed anesthesiology boards, it's not a requirement in the 1970s.

Once, in the locker room I overheard one of the nurses complaining about Joseph Panute.

"That ignorant little Napoleon," she fumed. "Where does he get off at, givin' me a ration? He's tellin' me to do somethin' I know is not right and he can't even pass his boards! I got my license to protect! I told Lillie that too, an' she's a sweetheart of a supervisor. She backed me right up!"

Whenever I see him swaggering down the corridor I try to be heading in another direction. I'm particularly uneasy because of an incident that happened a short time prior to Chief Sing's death. Panute was over in room 2 giving anesthesia to a seventy-two-year-old man whose abdominal aortic aneurysm was being repaired. It wasn't ruptured yet. The complex operation had been going on all morning. I was working in another room. I'd just finished with a cystoscopy patient when Dr. Sing came in and whispered in my ear.

"They're having trouble in OR 2 and Shillinger is calling for you."

I balked. I didn't want to get involved in that volatile situation.

"Chief, can't you stay in there and help Panute?"

"I can't. I need to be free for emergencies. We've got too many rooms running right now. Come on, Emily. See what you can do to appease that surgeon."

"Okay. It might not be pretty," I muttered under my breath.

I reluctantly grabbed my equipment and moved toward the action.

On the way, I couldn't help enjoying a little ego trip. The chief of surgery was calling for me. How 'bout that!

When I entered room 2, Panute had his back turned, but the surgeon looked up. His big gloved hands were immersed in the oozing field of guts and crimson sponges.

"Get us straightened out here, Emily! His pressure keeps going too high, then too low and his blood's dark at times." Red-faced, he jerked his head sideways toward Panute. "I don't know what's going on up at that end of the table."

Panute snorted. Grudgingly, the sweating anesthesiologist mumbled vital information to me about the drugs and fluids he gave. I quickly checked the deteriorating man under the bloodstained drapes. His face was ashen. I walked around the room, calculating how much blood was in the suction bottles, sponges, drapes and on the floor. Past experience showed that guys usually have a tough time estimating blood-loss. Females seem a lot better at it, maybe because we do more cooking or something?

I notified the circulating nurse, "Wilma, get four more units of blood up right away. We'll give some albumin in the meantime, to keep him going." The woman looked questioningly at Dr. Panute for approval.

"Nah! He had plenty already!"

The irate surgeon's head popped up. "Go ahead and do it, Wilma! Get that blood up here!" he commanded.

In silent fury, Panute stomped out of the room.

Quickly I sent a blood specimen from the patient to the lab to check hemoglobin levels, which proved my assessment correct. The next transfusion stabilized the patient's circulatory system and the rest of the procedure was uneventful. We still had the issue of Dr. Panute. He'd been humiliated, with his judgment being questioned. The whole OR was abuzz about it.

Ever since Dr. Sing's cardiac arrest I've had an eerie feeling about it. And now Dr. Joseph Panute is my new boss.

DANCING

MY STOMACH HAS butterflies. I haven't been dancing in a very long time. My hair is swept up and back and the new padded bra nicely fills out the silky scoop neck blouse. I feel a tickle as the little black skirt flutters over my hips and thighs when I twirl. My image in the full length mirror on the back of my bedroom door delights me.

John, in a dark sport jacket and turtleneck, arrives right on time and after a brief introduction to Miss Ellis and the children we head out the door.

The disco is vibrating with the beat of a '70s top hit and the dim lighting is punctuated by a strobe-flashing lighted dance floor.

John is a good dancer. At first I maintain a little space between us but after a couple of whiskey sours we begin to really dance, our bodies blending gracefully as the music carries us into a sensual celebration. Simon and Garfunkel's "Bridge over Troubled Water" mirrors my feelings. All our troubles forgotten, we don't need to talk. Our only fascination is the pure joy of dancing together.

When the evening is over we're still strangers but the satisfying evening has healed some of our pain, John's from Vietnam and mine from my failed marriage. The haunting song "Stairway to Heaven" flows around us from the radio as we sit close together on the leather seat of his Dodge. It seems natural for us to kiss now. His arms encircle me and our lips touch gently, then hungrily. The windows fog up from our bodies still warm from the dancing.

Later I wonder. Could he tell I was wearing a padded bra?

The package is on the doorstep when I get home from work.

Finally! I've been waiting for weeks. Now maybe I can accomplish something. Let's see what it looks like. I dash to my bedroom and lock the door, though no one else is home. Ripping open the package, I hold up the shocking-pink device and study it closely. The two six-inch long pieces are connected by a large metal spring. Quickly scanning the instructions, I place one hand on each side of the plastic device and rhythmically press the pieces together as hard as I can. It squeaks a little each time I compress the spring.

I better stand in front of the mirror to see if I'm doing it right.

The sudden sight of a purse-lipped young woman intensely working the breast developer makes me snicker out loud.

But if this works it'll be worth it!

APRON REMOVAL

I HAVE ONLY one surgery scheduled for the whole day, which means it's gonna be a long one. The schedule says, "Removal of Penniculus." That's a new one on me. I better look this up. Dr. Chester is at the scrub sink talking with Mark, his surgical resident. As I approach, the balding plastic surgeon turns to me.

"We've literally got our work cut out for us today, Emily. Our patient has done an amazing job of losing over two hundred pounds. She's down to 220 from 440."

I purse my lips in a big circle. "Wow."

"Now she has a big fatty apron from her shrunken abdomen that's draping down to her knees. We're going to remove it."

So that's what a panniculus is. This ought to be a real project. Now I understand why it's the only case scheduled in my room.

Margie Angelino is thirty-two, about five feet four inches tall, and except for the loose hanging flesh on her upper arms and belly, she is in good health. I feel a lot of compassion for Margie. She must have missed out on a lot of chocolate doughnuts in the last two years. She's embarrassed and her pretty face flushes as she says, "Dr. Chester told me I'm going to lose quite a few pounds today, maybe even thirty or forty. I can't wait."

"You'll have to go shopping for some new clothes. That'll be fun." I can relate to this with some envy. Shopping for clothes is how Michelle and I often reward ourselves for all our hard work. We have endurance, too. We'll try on clothes until we physically cannot carry another armload into the dressing room.

After Margie is anesthetized, the stocky little Dr. Chester and the tall resident pull the sheet away to expose her pale torso. The large flap of flesh is sagging over the sides of the operating table, all dimpled and wrinkled. I stare over the anesthesia screen. How are they going to do this? The doctors position two IV poles up against the table, one on either side of Margie's belly. They then place a heavy rod across the tops of the two upright poles and secure it with bandage roll. With the cross-rod suspended horizontally across the table at the level of Margie's bellybutton, Mark grabs the rod and pulls, his biceps bulging as he tests their construction job.

"That's real strong, Dr. C. Could probably take a couple hundred pounds."

"Let's scrub her up, then. Okay, Emily?"

"She's all set. You can start." I turn the gas up higher and peek over my screen again. I can't take my eyes off the vast glacier-like mound of flesh sliding back and forth to the two doctors' vigorous iodine cleansing.

Keeping everything sterile, Dr. Chester picks up what looks like a steel tow hook, grabs a handful of belly and quickly skewers it, forcing the sharp point all the way through until the bloody tip is coming out the other side. Mark threads thick ropelike bandage through the loop and hands it up and over the horizontal rod to the surgeon.

"Okay, Mark, come over here and help me." The two men slowly pull on the towrope bandage, dragging the hook and the quivering mass of belly up toward the ceiling and they secure it. Next they carefully slather the mountain of flesh with orange antiseptic. The whole team watches in fascination. The glistening ghoulish appendage hanging there seems like a horror movie scene.

Now the real work begins. As she sleeps peacefully, Margie's airborne apron gradually loses its hold on her. After hours of sweating under the hot lights, the two men finally sever the last strand and heave the massive belly-buttoned porterhouse onto the waiting scale.

It weighs forty-six pounds. Quickly they turn their full attention to the gaping hole that remains in their patient's abdomen. Some initial heavy-duty stitches are placed to align both sides of the vast incision and they begin the tedious task of performing a plastic closure that Margie will find cosmetically acceptable.

As they work, I begin to prepare the drugs I'll need to reverse the young woman's anesthesia at the end of the surgery. My eyes twinkle as I imagine the reaction my nurse friend Michelle would have if she could see this unusual procedure.

When Dr. Chester and Mark complete their handiwork the patient actually has a lovely hourglass figure. The men are jubilant. Me, not so much, as I notice the hair-line. Her belly is pulled together with the pubic hair line on the lower flap almost all the way up to her breasts.

The next morning the resident whispers to me, "I just came back from checking our patient's wound. Wherever I touched her, I violated her!"

"Maybe she can have electrolysis?"

Hmmm.

BUST DEVELOPMENT

I'M STICKING TO it with at least one fifteen-minute session every day. Each time I work with the pink bust developer I wonder if anything has changed yet. After several weeks, I finally get up my courage.

Today is the day.

After making sure the door is locked, I slowly unbutton my blouse. The blood is pounding hard in my neck. I sit down on the bed and take a deep breath.

This is too weird.

I've never actually studied my nude body in the mirror before.

Hot with embarrassment, I slowly slip off the cotton shirt and unhook my stiff padded bra. There's no turning back now. I have to look.

As I stand up, the bra slides to the floor. Taking a deep breath, I move in front of the full-length mirror. Head down, I focus on the pink device my hands are clutching.

"Squeak! Squeak! Squeak!" The bust developer sounds like a distressed bird. Slowly I lift my head and stare.

Look at that scrawny chest and those pokey little nipples!

I hate it.

The squeaking stops. I toss the thing down. But in that quick movement I see something else. The reflection I catch in the mirror is sensuous and rather lovely. Yes, the breasts are small, yet in that instant of looking objectively, I see they are full and young, more like a teenager than a mother of three children. I have to admit that the reflected bosom is perfectly proportioned for my small frame. I wrap my arms around my nakedness and grin. My reflection grins back.

IMPURE THOUGHTS

JOHN AND I have been dating for several months, and we always have a good time together, but I'm aware of his hungry need for more. He's shared very little of his service in Vietnam with me, but I know he has nightmares. He warned me never to come near him if he falls asleep. I should just stand across the room and call his name. He told me his first wife left him because he almost choked her to death one night before he realized he wasn't in the jungle fighting a Vietcong soldier.

Although John is gentle with me he sure is persistent. Lately I'm having a heck of a time wheedling out of the kissing and groping sessions. He's also been leaving a letter on the front windshield of my car at night. It's there when I leave for work in the morning. I sit on the john at work and read John's love notes. If he only knew!

I do enjoy the attention. I'm starved for affection. But I can't seem to let my guard down. I just dread the feeling of getting attached to this guy.

What's wrong with me? Could it be my Catholic upbringing? Come on now! I have three kids! I'm divorced, for God's sake! I haven't been to church since I went on birth control after Amanda was born.

Well, that could be my problem. Who knows what fifteen years of Catholic school did to my subconscious. I think back to the day my first-grade teacher Sister Josephine stared down that beak-like nose and loudly proclaimed, "You are committing a Mortal Sin if you have Impure Thoughts."

I was only five but I definitely knew what Mortal Sin meant. You will burn in the Fires of Hell. But what were Impure Thoughts? I became alarmed. Maybe I already had one and didn't even know it! Sister Josephine never did explain what "Impure Thoughts" are. When I got home I asked my mom. She just kept folding the laundry. I didn't think she even heard me, except that her face turned real pink. Finally she sputtered, "It's like when you go to the bathroom." Then she snatched up the towels and skittered out of the room before I could say another word.

Well, it just didn't make any sense to me. I figured, God made us have to go to the toilet. How can it be a Mortal Sin? So there was only one thing I could do. I decided to stop my thoughts. Stop my imagination! That way, whatever Impure Thoughts were, I wouldn't be having any.

Back in 1938 I was my mother's first baby. She must have had a rough time. My body is still a little crooked and asymmetrical. But that didn't deter my father. She had six more of us in the next nine years before her uterus revolted. Years later, Mom shared that she really wanted to be a nun. But when the convent turned her down for health reasons, the family priest told her to get married and have lots of babies.

As a kid, anger was a close friend of mine. Because of it, I would almost always get my way at home. My younger brothers and sisters were afraid of me and my mother's gentle spirit was no match for the raging volcano inside me. Of course, Dad always loved me no matter what I did. After all, I was just like him.

Our early childhood was filled with fun trips to the county park for picnics and fishing trips to a local creek. We called it the "crick." Many evenings Dad herded us into the family Chevy and drove over to the Robertsboro train station to see the 6:10 come in. That was a real event. Those old steam engines are a thing of the past now.

Almost imperceptible at first, the *chuga-chuga* got louder and louder, closer and closer until we finally spotted the big black monster charging around the bend. The massive engine, belching its mushroom cloud of white steam, would screech to a halt right in front of us. The 6:10 from Toledo was always right on time. The engineer waved at our familiar entourage, then sounded an ear-shattering blast of the horn. He'd chuckle as the baby shrieked.

Mike the patriarch, ruled without much consideration for what Mom thought. But our parents loved us, and only Mom's miscarriages and hemorrhages stopped them from producing more little O'Briens. Whenever Gram came to help with a new baby, friction between her and Dad erupted into caustic remarks and arguments. Gram was not a "yes" person like her daughter. She refused to be intimidated. Mom was caught miserably in the middle. Her milk production would slow and the baby would cry and cry. Eventually when Gram left, peace was restored. Or so it seemed.

One day when I was in second grade, I arrived home from school to find the house repugnant with cloying Prince Machiavelli. Someone had given the perfume to Mom as a gift years before, but she never used it. It was basically a dust-catcher on top of her dresser. I followed the scent and discovered her upstairs, decked out in a sheer low-cut red nightgown, black stockings and high heels. Around her neck and wrists jewelry jangled with every move. She didn't notice me as she admired herself in the mirror. Appalled, I slipped away and tiptoed up the stairs to the attic bedroom I shared with my sisters. I hid there until Dad came home from work.

I heard him shout at her so I crept down the stairs to peek. Ignoring his contorted face she sauntered up to him and ran her hands through his hair. He grabbed her hands and tried to talk quietly and sweetly. But his simple wife was gone and in her place was a woman he may have fantasized about. It was not the modest girl he married. On that horrible day Mom was admitted to a mental institution. We didn't see her again for many months.

I remember cooking for the family, big pots of mashed potatoes. Gram praised my ironing, so I still love to do ironing. Over the next twenty years Mom was afflicted with "nervous breakdowns" several times. Funny thing is, the psychiatrist always spent more time talking with Dad than her.

Back then Dad was working as a sports reporter at the local newspaper. The Catholic nuns who taught at our school were regularly favored by crates of oranges and grapefruits, Mike's way of making sure his children were well taken care of.

Music lessons were part of our grade school life. I took piano lessons. My sister Kay took violin.

When I was seven, Sister Erma the music teacher was also my third grade teacher. She was quite strict. If a pupil got a math problem incorrect, there would be corporal punishment. The whole class feared arithmetic period, especially me. One day I got all twelve answers wrong. Along with the several other losers I stood in front of the class. The nun worked her way down the line with a wooden ruler in her hand.

"How many incorrect answers? Three? Put out your hands." *WHACK! WHACK! WHACK!* I close my eyes for an instant and the flooding memory actually recreates the smell of chalk as I envision Sister moving closer to me.

Finally the black-hooded, rosary-wearing terrorist stood right in front of me. I couldn't believe this was happening. Hangdog, I searched her grim face but found no sign of reprieve. I got twelve wrong. Slow, slowly I held out both of my trembling hands, palms up. My eyes scrunched shut.

WHACK! WHACK! WHACK! WHACK! WHACK! WHACK! WHACK! WHACK! WHACK! WHACK! WHACK! WHACK!

I have no memory of the rest of the day until my father picked me up from school. When he saw my face his eyes widened.

"Emily! What's wrong?"

Tears streamed down my cheeks as I struggled to hold back the scream in my chest. He took my hot swollen hands in his cool ones. His head was down, but I could see his eyes were moist.

"Are you sure you didn't do something bad?" But he already knew the answer. Those nuns taught him too.

He'd bully Mom, but he could never confront a nun. All my hopes for justice were dashed. In fact, he doubled the fruit delivery to the convent. That's all he could think to do. But worse than that, I continued to take piano lessons with this same hard-faced teacher.

Every Tuesday afternoon I walked from my classroom across the school yard to the convent front door. A nun took me down the basement stairs to the musty piano room. Soon Sister Erma would rush in, her frown already in place. Sitting on the piano bench, I would stare at my white knuckles knotted in my lap while she started the metronome. *Click. Click. Click.* Then she would speak loud and slow, as if she thought I had poor hearing or something. "All right, Emily. Let's start with page twenty two. You were supposed to practice that piece this week." Pond's Cold Cream and some other acrid scent emitted from under her bib as she rifled through my music book. I tentatively positioned my right index finger over middle C. The notes on the page would blur before me and fade in and out. The question was never out of my awareness. Will she use her ruler on me again?

Sister could barely contain her impatience as I'd bungle the notes. The click-clicking never synchronized with my piano playing, but surely it was replicating my bounding heart. At last the lesson would be over and my uptight fingers felt reprieved for another week.

Not once during my four years of piano lessons with Sister Erma did she hit me. She apparently saved that for the arithmetic class. Unfortunately my little hands never got over the dread of the ruler. No subtle melodies were ever forthcoming. I only seemed to produce plain pounding sounds.

Even though we brothers and sisters were living together, I guess we were not really close. That is we didn't know how to talk to each other. Communication amounted to either teasing or arguing whose turn it was for the one bathroom. If two of us passed on the street, we didn't even acknowledge each other. But we did love each other. One day my sister Kay, fourteen months younger than me, was getting beat up by some neighborhood boys. When I saw this my rage flared and I ripped into them, giving one a bloody nose. They ran away bawling. I helped my sister up, brushed her off and we went our separate ways. It was never mentioned again.

At thirteen I applied for my first job, babysitting. Dad drove me to the interview. It was a split-level home in a new development. Mrs. Yeager had two boys, a two-year-old and a three-month old. Dad, as always, took control of the conversation, praising his daughter for all her accomplishments and experience with babies. I was appalled. Who was he talking about? Naturally I got hired on the spot. When I reported for my first day Mrs. Yeager handed me the baby.

"Here he is, dear. Give him his bath."

I froze. "But-I-I-I don't know how."

"What? Your father said you had lots of experience!"

"Well, my mother always took care of the babies at our house. I got to do the ironing and stuff."

Chagrined, the woman took back her little one. "I guess I'll have to do the bath myself. Humph. Can you at least fold the laundry?"

Mrs. Yeager was too intimidated by my dad to fire me. She had no choice but to make the best of it. Thus began my gradual training in the care of two young children. Before long her patience paid off. I became a capable manager of the household and the parents were comfortable leaving me with their children while they went partying late into the night. Sometimes I stayed overnight, sleeping on a cot in the baby's room. I was grateful. I got away from home for a night and was earning $9 a week!

After high school graduation came I got accepted into a three-year hospital school of nursing. To pay the $300 tuition, I worked as a waitress that summer. This was another job my influential father got for me. By now Dad had been promoted to editor of the local weekly newspaper, and he wielded power over the town in not so subtle ways. It was common knowledge that if ever a member of Mike O'Brien's family was slighted, the offender would be treated to some unpleasant coverage in the Robertsboro Herald.

Poor Mr. Johnson was coerced into hiring me as a waitress in his stylish restaurant even though I had zero experience. On my first day the other waitresses gave me a haphazard ten-minute training before the patrons arrived. It was Easter Sunday.

Taking customers' dinner orders was difficult for a girl with no social skills. I didn't even know to greet and smile graciously. But I felt proud the first time I balanced a big tray laden with seven turkey dinners on my shoulder just like the experienced waitresses. Unfortunately, as I entered the dining room through the swinging door, I miscalculated. The door slammed into the back of my tray causing all seven dinners to slide off and splash with a terrible clatter at the feet of Mr. Johnson. His impeccable navy pinstripe suit was plastered with mashed potatoes and gravy.

What a mess. I watched frozen in fear as his face turned beet red. His fiery temper was famous among the waitresses. By sheer force of will he managed to contain himself as the girls scurried to scrape the gunk off his trousers and sop up the mess on the floor. When he finally could speak he snarled to the old-timers, "*Show her how to do it.*" Later one of them confided to me that anyone else would have been fired on the spot. I never became competent, but I did earn the $300 by summer's end and entered nursing school in September.

Shyness impeded my progress with boys. There also was my flat chest. Luckily, I discovered padded bras. In 1953 they were quite stiff and cardboard-like. Sometimes one side would become dented, causing a crater effect on the front of my sweater. Hugging invariably was the cause. One time, a girlfriend got me a date with an older guy. We went out in his snazzy car. He wanted to neck but I fended him off nicely. When I got home my left A-cup was dented. I was mortified. He knew my secret and I never felt him touch my chest. He didn't ask me out again. Neither did any of his friends.

We always had an older teenager, a foster child living with us to help mom. Dolores and I shared a room. When I was thirteen she became aware that I knew nothing about the birds and the bees. One hot night we sat in our third floor room trying to catch a breeze by the open window. We could see the high neon Ice Never Fails sign from a mile away. In the dark, she graphically whispered the anatomical facts of how babies are created. I couldn't believe it.

"NO NO NO! My parents would NEVER do THAT!" I hissed at her. Dolores laughed. "You wouldn't be here if they didn't!"

None of my girlfriends knew either. The responsibility of educating them fell on me. That was a hoot. They were just as disgusted as me.

Enough of this ancient history. Here I am now, dating a nice guy. When it comes to takin' my clothes off with this guy, something is holding me back. After all, I'm a nurse! We're supposed to be good with nudity an' stuff, aren't we?

Just the same, all the stress at work makes me want to fall into his big strong arms and be protected forever. What I need is some good old-fashioned comforting.

I just wish I could feel some real passion. I gotta work on those impure thoughts more, I guess. Never mind Going to Hell.

HOW 10 WE MET

AFTER OUR MARRIAGE disintegrated, Paul eventually landed on the coast of Maryland. The original "other woman" became ancient history. He was living the life he'd dreamed about, totally free to work when he wanted and play when he liked. He rented a shack in the low-rent district and worked building and selling small custom sailboats. Janice moved in a couple years back. Skinny, tough and tanned, she seemed to relish their simple existence. She grew some vegetables out back. Sometimes she'd catch fish which she would cook over a fire outdoors in summer. In cold weather everything got stewed in an old black pot on the two-burner hotplate in the hovel.

One summer I let the kids visit their dad and Janice for a couple of weeks. They returned subdued and bedraggled, guardedly sharing some of their adventures. I worried about what they didn't want to talk about.

He gave no financial help to support the children. Overwhelmed and desperate, I harassed him until finally he signed the house over to me, mortgage and all. Since then there has been very little communication.

Until now.

I arrive home to the jangling of the phone.

"Hello?"

"It's me. Paul."

I stuff my instant wave of annoyance and quip, "What's up?"

45

"I got a little problem. It's called melanoma."

My heart twists in my chest. "What? What do you mean?" I can feel his extreme distress.

"Had a mole removed from my chest last week. Doc says I got a level four melanoma. "Wants to sign me up for some death counseling." Fright makes his voice sound tight and high.

"That can't be right!" I blurt. "You've got to come up here and see a REAL doctor, Paul. That guy sounds like an idiot!"

"Well, all right." I hear the relief in his voice when I say I'll help him. He wasn't sure I would.

"We'll leave right away. Janice and the dog are coming with me."

Level four melanoma on the chest wall is something to be reckoned with. After hanging up I think about what to do.

I'll talk to Shillinger about it, see what he thinks. There's no health insurance, of course. This is real serious.

I break into a sweat.

Oh, no! John and I have a date tonight. I have a flash of my luscious new undies from Gimbels.

I can't do this. Not with Paul and Janice arriving tonight. I detect a rush of relief. I won't be taking those black panties off this evening after all.

When I call him to discuss suspending our dating for a while, John is incredulous.

"How can he just come barging back in on your life, Emily? I thought it was you an' me now. How could you let him?"

I'm not too surprised at his heated reaction.

"He's real sick, John! And he's my children's father. I have to do what I can for him."

"All righty then. Sounds like you made your choice. I see your true colors now. I'm just your stupid lackey. I guess you'll be jumpin' back in the sack with him now."

"No, John, it's not like that at all!"

46

"Just forget it. I'm fed up with trying to make it with a frigid woman anyhow!" He rants on and on, ending with, "I'm movin' on! Don't call me." The loud CLICK on the phone is the final note.

I realize I'm trembling. I've never seen this side of John. This is not my man after all. Good riddance.

Dr. Shillinger proposes a bilateral axillary dissection. The surgeon puts it in plain words. "We need to get all those lymph nodes out from your armpits. That's where it will spread next. Let's get a jump on it." After a brief discussion Paul and Janice agree. The operation is scheduled for the next day.

Before the surgery, Paul sits upright on the stretcher inside the OR. He chides me for introducing him to my coworkers as "my ex."

He pleads, "Couldn't you just say 'my former husband'?" Then he asks me to kiss him. I struggle to find some compassion for this man who caused me so many years of grief. His eyes are ready to overflow with tears. After a long hesitation I force myself to hurriedly give him a peck on his bearded cheek. I can hardly stand it.

How did we ever end up like this?

In the summer of 1955, I discovered the joy of roller-skating, and that also was when Paul and I met. I had just graduated from high school. Every Friday evening, Dad drove my two sisters and me to the skating rink. With my first loop around the rink, all the cares in my world disappeared. For three blissful hours the music would carry my heart to a place of enchantment as my body glided round and round the sleek circle.

A boy, tall and blue eyed, asked me to skate with him. It was Paul. He began to teach me to dance on skates. We moved together gracefully to a slow song in the gentle darkness as the mirror ball in the ceiling spun magical sparks all around us. He even laughed when I accidentally tripped him and the two of us were splayed out all over the floor as the other skaters dodged around us.

I was not concerned about him denting my A-cups. He was just as shy and awkward as me. He never tried to touch or kiss me. We were friends. In this way, Dad got used to seeing this lanky fellow every Friday. Then Dad remembered working with a guy named Harry Summerfield years before. Paul checked with his dad who confirmed that they had history together. So there was no problem when Paul asked if he could pick me up at home so we could skate on an extra night. For the rest of the summer we two seventeen-year-olds skated three evenings a week. Little by little we came to care for each other.

Nursing school in 1955 was "school" for the first six months. After that, we were on the wards every day, taking care of patients. Each morning as we climbed the hospital's cold marble stairs, the same prayer flashed through my petrified being, "God, help me to not hurt anybody."

I couldn't tremble due to the strict uniform dress code enforced by the Sisters of Mercy. Girdles must be worn. Girdled at five feet eight inches tall and 118 pounds, believe me when I say that nothing on my lower body was free to tremble. Or jiggle. The sisters knew what they are doing. On various occasions in the male ward, a groper on the other side of the curtain would try to pinch my bottom, but to no avail. That area was stiff as a board and definitely unsqueezable.

In 1958, we senior student nurses had the narcotic closet key where the little bottle of Paregoric was secured. Paregoric is camphorated tincture of opium. When suffering from menstrual cramps while on duty, a tiny teaspoonful would relax the uterus and coat a nurse's entire body in a soothing warmth that made the whole shift fly smoothly by, on wings of bliss.

In fact, the three years flew by, with many months of evening and night shifts. All three floors of the hospital were staffed by student nurses, with one RN covering the whole place each shift. During our stint at a psychiatric hospital, the long hat pin on our nurse's cap became a possible weapon if a deranged patient should grab it. So no hat pins were allowed, and no attracting attention by jingling keys. We played cards with murderers during the day and shared the kitchen with rats at night.

Another rotation was a neurologic ward where we cared for third-stage syphilis patients and quadriplegics. One new admission I washed was a man who had not gotten clean for many years. The crusted dirt on his feet was like cement.

Paul and I were inseparable on my one and a half days off each week. We liked to hang out at his house while his parents were at work in the candy shop out back. His mother had her own candy making business and they were too busy to notice all the time we spent in Paul's bedroom. When summer came, the family left for an extended trip, leaving him home alone. What a sensual summer it was. We'd sunbathe nude on the upper deck. We'd take showers together. Neither of us had ever been close to the opposite sex before, so our exploratory sessions were gentle and circumspect. He was never the instigator. Even though Paul was not a Catholic, he respected my belief that I would go to Hell if we had sexual intercourse. And we didn't.

Paul joined the air force and was stationed in Texas. We corresponded every day and he sent photos. During my last two years in nursing school, we became even closer despite being apart. When I was about to graduate, he got word that he'd be transferred abroad soon, so we decided to get married. This decision would fulfill my two greatest desires, to travel and to have sexual intercourse.

When he got home on leave three days before the wedding, we had not seen each other for six months. Both of us were in turmoil with wedding preparations, but the night before our wedding his bedroom became our sanctuary. We held each other close. The kissing began gently at first, but quickly became urgent, our breath coming fast. I don't even remember getting undressed, but when our naked bodies touched, Paul was unable to resist my virginal being any more. Crazed with passion, we made love for the first time. Exquisite. Painful. Hot. Velvet.

Now what to do with the bloody sheets?

That night I learned how my medical dictionary didn't tell the complete story of sexual intercourse. The book never said anything about going in and out, in and out.

My wedding day was supposed to be happy. I was in a total panic. I must not receive the Sacrament of Matrimony with this Mortal Sin on my conscience. I was too ashamed to confess to our parish priest what happened the night before, so Paul and I drove miles to find a priest who didn't know me, so I could receive the Sacrament of Confession and have my sin forgiven. I remember with amusement the priest's asking, "This was really your 'first' time?"

Our wedding day was a blur. We just wanted to get it over with and get away from all the relatives for a three day honeymoon at the beach. It was August and ninety eight degrees out, but we spent most of the time in bed. Then Paul traveled alone back to his air force base.

Right after our wedding Gram had rectal cancer operated on. I guess all those Milk of Magnesia pills finally caught up with her. She used to pretend they were candy, to make us kids take them. To this day I still hate peppermint. Anyway, she had an abdomino-perineal resection which means they removed her rectum and gave her a colostomy. In my mind this was worse than death. But for Gram, after years of constipation, it was a pleasure. It was right in the front and only needed irrigation every other day. She's the only person I ever heard of who was absolutely delighted to have a colostomy.

I took care of Gram in the hospital and then joined Paul in Riverside California while he trained for his next assignment. This was my first airplane trip. Commercial jet flights were not available yet, so my journey took all day. It was an eye opener for me to see the United States, while cruising at 350 miles an hour, at an altitude of ten thousand to twenty-five thousand feet, across the cities, vast plains, lakes and mountain ranges. So spectacular!

While we were stationed there I worked at the local hospital. I had to walk the fourteen blocks to and from work, enjoying the forty degree temperatures at 7:00 a.m. and the one hundred and four degrees when I got off at 3:00 p.m. I delivered a patient's surprisingly speedy baby all by myself. Too soon, Paul was transferred and we traveled back across the country by Greyhound bus. What a hellish five days and nights we spent sitting up, huddled hornily together, touching each other under cover of our coats, surrounded by many stinky folks and crying babies.

As the bus had no rest room, the three twenty-minute stops a day meant that one of us got the food, the other used the gas station restroom.

Paul flew to England. The air force would not pay his wife's travel expenses across the ocean. So I moved back in with Mom and Dad and got a nursing position at a Toledo medical center, in their ICU. In a few weeks I saved enough money to buy a plane ticket to Great Britain.

Again I flew all day, this time on the precursor of the jet, a turbo-prop. I think the racket of the engines for nine hours affected my hearing permanently. At first I was thrilled to be visiting a foreign country and getting to see the world. But I'll never forget my first terrified day in a strange land, all alone in a hotel room. After a few hours, I was starving. With no idea what time it was—my watch was still set on US Eastern Standard Time—or when my husband would return, I ventured out on the street. They might have been speaking English, but the cockney dialect was so strong I couldn't understand a word. I wandered around, staring at shoe and clothing shops, wondering what the strange price tags meant. I came to a shop selling sandwiches, already made up and wrapped in paper. This should be easy. The clerk asked me for "Sempin ape-knee." "Sempin ape-knee," she repeated sharply. I gave her a handful of money and took the sandwich. Later I found out she was asking me for seven pence, half-penny.

Before I arrived, Paul wanted to surprise me. He used our meager wedding checks as down payment on a little red sports car. When I arrived a month later, the Berkeley was his big treat. Unfortunately, he had not known how high auto insurance would be on such a fancy automobile. The car loan, insurance payments and rent took his whole salary. We did need a car, and he was so delighted. How could I object? Anyway, I was used to the man buying the transportation. My dad always chose the car in our family and it would always render my mother speechless. Especially the time he brought the avant-garde Edsel home.

In Shefford, about forty miles north of London, we rented a little cottage. It had four rooms: two tiny bedrooms upstairs, a living room and kitchen downstairs. The kitchen had a bathtub in it covered with a board that we used as a table, except when we took a bath. And we did take *a* bath. It took forever to heat up lots of water on the two burner electric stove. When the tub was filled, we'd light up the stinky kerosene heater and quickly strip down in the fifty degree Fahrenheit kitchen. Together, we carefully folded our lanky bodies into the claw foot tub, our heads at opposite ends, legs and feet intertwined in the middle. It wasn't very romantic. We soon decided the blokes had it right. One bath a week is plenty.

Paul worked shifts, leaving me alone at night most of the time. With good reason the locals were not friendly toward American service people. Some of the guys would impregnate their daughters, return to the States and forget all about it. For the first time, I experienced being a hated minority.

Our toilet stall was outside, against the back wall of the house. A large ceramic water tank hung over your head, with a pull chain to flush. I didn't pay much attention to it until one day while sitting there, I saw a fly get stuck in a gigantic cobweb right over my head. Suddenly a fist-size spider galloped out from behind that tank, grabbed the fly and scampered back out of sight. Thus began many years of constipation. You better believe I especially never used it after dark. Under our creaky old bed was a "honey pot." I'll say no more.

I couldn't get a nursing job on our base as I had planned, because there was no hospital. I couldn't work at a British hospital as I was not licensed in the United Kingdom. I didn't care. I wanted to have a baby. After a few months I did become pregnant. But instead of the joy I expected, what I felt was total dread. How could we care for a tiny infant? The only heat in our cottage came from the living room fireplace, when we finally could get the coal lit. We had no hot water and no refrigeration.

Paul and I barely had money for the quarter-pound of ground beef I bought daily to create some gourmet recipe from my Fanny Farmer cookbook.

Twice a month we managed to save up eleven pence to buy a pint of hard cider from the local pub, go home and play poker. It was fun for me when, after a few ounces of the liquor, Paul always began to lose.

The little red Berkeley needed plenty of attention. It was a race car, not designed for street use. Every three thousand miles, the engine ran badly and constantly stalled out, leaving us stranded. This entailed the complete tear-down of the motor and a scraping of the carbon off the head, whatever that meant. He kept all his tools in the car. I spent many hours sitting in the grass alongside a country lane, sometimes in the dark, rain or fog, listening to sheep bleat as Paul serviced his bloody car. Often the process was done in our eight foot by nine foot living room, the greasy parts spread out on newspapers all over the floor. On occasion, his buddies and their wives stopped by to observe and chat. The girls were horrified at the spectacle, but what could I do?

Alfred Hitchcock's horror movie "Psycho" came to the local theatre and we splurged to see the one and only movie in our two years in England. I had never seen a horror film before, and it had a dire impact on me. I became pervaded by fear, especially during the long cold nights alone while Paul was at the base. I had been ignoring my pregnancy, but as my shape began to change, reality became devastatingly clear. Panic overcame me. How I could adequately care for a tiny infant in this squalor? Hopelessness finally pushed me over the edge. I screamed and cried hysterically. When Paul tried I would not be comforted.

At four months gestation something changed inside me. The fetus couldn't stand it either. My swelling girth subsided. Then the bleeding started. My uterus got rid of the dead little one.

At the hospital, I forgot to ask them to baptize the tiny person curled among the clots on the striped towel between my legs. The next day another distraught young woman had a miscarriage. When she was admitted, she cried out to the nurse that there was someone else's fetus on a striped towel lying on the floor in the corner of the examining room. I cried for a long time. My baby had become trash on the floor.

I don't know whether Paul was sad about losing his child. We never talked about it. I never saw him shed a tear. After a couple months, in an effort to console myself I went to join the choir at the local Catholic Church. The priest and choir were civil enough. When rehearsal was over, Father encouraged everyone to practice the hymns at home. When I started toward the door he stopped me. "Oh no, not you. Leave our hymn book here, please." The other members glanced at each other smugly and shuffled out.

I never returned. Now I was truly alone in my grief.

When we first arrived in Great Britain, I had applied for a British RN license. A year later, it arrived in the mail. Just in time, as we needed survival money. I pulled myself together and got a job at the Bedford General Hospital. I worked as a "sister" in the private wing. Nobody expected me to actually do work. Current Doris Day movies told the story of how we "Yanks" lived. But work I did, even orienting the staff to the new clear plastic IV tubing, which we'd been using at home.

I tried not to be homesick. The British newspapers kept us up to date on the Russian Sputnik's short space flight, and John F. Kennedy was running for President. He won, though we couldn't vote for him from England.

The first British super highway opened, the M-1. Back home we were used to speed limits of fifty-five miles per hour. On the M-1 the sky was the limit. Jaguar owners had been waiting for this, and we also had to take our little sports car for a spin. What a mess. The highway was littered with all manner of collapsed vehicles of various ages and degrees of rust. Tires were flying off cars all around us. Most folks' old junkers were not meant to go one hundred miles an hour, but the blokes had to give it a go.

After two years Paul was flown stateside. He shipped his sacrosanct sports car home but we had no funds for me so Paul's father lent me just enough money. Ship was cheaper so I traveled alone on the colossal steamer SS *United States*. It was December and rough seas kept most of the passengers ill. I'd gotten medicine for nausea from my British physician, so I never missed a meal. Thalidomide it was called. (Two years later it was pulled off the market as many British women who took it for nausea during pregnancy gave birth to severely deformed children. It had never been approved for use in the US.)

After a six day stormy north Atlantic passage, at crimson dawn I clung to the icy railing on the windswept deck. Tears of joy and relief ran down my frosty cheeks. I tried to hold back the sobs as we glided past the Statue of Liberty into New York Harbor on December 15, 1959. I was home! My whole family greeted me at the dock and laughed at my British accent.

We were living in Robertsboro only two weeks when I got pregnant. I was already working in the Intensive Care Unit again. One day, leaning my still flat belly against the nurses' station desk during morning report I felt the unmistakable flutter kick of my eight-week-old fetus. My eyes glowed with love. I knew this would be a good one. And he was! Eight and one half pounds of energy and laughter entered our lives, perfectly healthy little Andrew. Thank goodness the Thalidomide I took two weeks before he was conceived was out of my system in time.

Three children and eleven years later, the marriage is over.

I come back to the present. Paul and I had a whole lifetime together it seems and now it is dead and gone.

Paul's lymph node procedure is uneventful and three days later he is discharged. Sitting on my couch, bandaged upper arms pressed against his sides, he gingerly pats his knee. "Scupper" his scruffy terrier leaps into his lap, yipping in pure delight. His master has returned.

"Now let's forget this ever happened," he says. Paul is glad it is over.

Janice's pinched expression reveals her concern. Chemotherapy is recommended but Paul refuses to put all those chemicals in his body. They head back home to Maryland.

11
POWER PLAY

DR. PANUTE HAS been Chief of Anesthesia for two months. One morning I'm in OR 1 setting up for a gynecological procedure. I like to work in this room because one whole wall is glass. None of the other operating rooms are open to the outside world. On sunny days we revel in the streams of golden sunlight that overpower the dreary fluorescent lighting. This second floor window offers a panoramic vista of the lush hospital grounds, including several tall deciduous trees close to the building. A chartreuse froth of spring growth is emerging from their dark branches. Millions of tiny brown seedpods are dangling on the tip of each branch, twinkling and twirling in the breeze. At a casual glance the trees seem almost humanoid, like a group of quivering giants staring into the room, ghoulishly anticipating what might happen next.

The OR table is set up with the patient's head toward the door on the opposite side from the window. The patient's feet point toward that glorious window. During certain vaginal and rectal procedures the patient's legs are hung up in the air, secured in stainless steel stirrups, leaving their genitals exposed to the surgeon. (And the window.) I sometimes wonder what it must look like to the birds and squirrels in those trees. What might they think about these various private parts all painted orange and shining under the big spotlight? Perhaps the animals see a big-eared creature with a small vertical mouth or maybe a monster with a dangling snout and acorn pouches. Dum-de-dum.

With my setup complete, I ask the circulating nurse, "Can you help me bring in the patient. She's a big woman."

Dr. Panute stops me at the doorway. "You're not planning to intubate her for this little vaginal repair, are you?"

"Yes, I am, Doctor. She's going to be in lithotomy and she's got a big belly."

He raises his voice. "Well I'm telling you! Don't intubate her. It's not necessary!"

I back into the OR. We're alone except for the scrub nurse, who pretends not to hear. Panute steps close to me, his nostrils flaring. I feel his garlicky breath on my face. Softly, urgently I appeal my case.

"I don't want to take a chance she might regurgitate and aspirate when her legs are up."

What is he thinking? He makes no sense at all.

Panute's face goes dark with wrath. He roars, "Who the hell do you think you are! You don't know anything! You're just plain stupid! Retarded!" He laughs in my face derisively, misting me with his spittle.

Softly I retort, "At least I passed my boards, Doctor."

"GET OUT! GET OUT, YOU BITCH!" My words stab him a sharp and deep wound. How could I know his secret? Panute lunges at me, arms flailing. "YOU BITCH! YOU'RE FIRED! GET THE HELL OUT OF HERE!"

I dart backward out of reach. I tear down the corridor and duck into the women's locker room. I lock myself inside one of the toilet stalls.

I stand rigid. Both buttocks are twitching. My chest heaves. I listen intently. I can hear the air whistling in and out of my nose.

He doesn't seem to be following me. Finally I plop down on the toilet seat, elbows resting on my knees. Holding my head in my hands, I inhale deeply. The dingy room reeks of sneakers and air freshener.

After a few minutes, the locker room door opens. "Are you all right, Emily?" The supervisor enters and begins to search the cramped room, stepping over scattered shoes and discarded scrubs. She peeks behind the center row of lockers.

"I'm in here, Lilly. Is it safe to come out? Where's that crazy man?"

Double-chinned, frumpy and mother hen-like, Lilly consistently looks after her staff. "He's doing your case in room 1. Come on outta that john, girl!"

We sit down close together on the narrow bench. The older woman puts her arm around my trembling shoulders. "I was afraid that little tin soldier would pull something like this."

I shake my head glumly.

"Looks like this is my last day at Robertsboro Hospital. He fired me. I didn't expect it to end like this. But he's dangerous and I can't work like that. I need to give safe anesthesia. I don't want to hurt a patient. I'm not gonna fight him, Lilly. I'm outta here!"

Lilly stands up. "I better get back out there to the war zone. No telling what else he's gonna pull. You and me, we've had some real good times. And you sure are good to those patients. I can't believe this, Emily." We hug distractedly.

At the hospital entrance my swollen eyes squint in the glare of pale sunlight. I feel breathless and disoriented. Panute's attack drained me.

Where will I go? What will I do? A tidal wave of fear inundates me.

I've got a mortgage to pay and three kids to feed. And no job.

How could I be fired for giving good safe anesthesia? Anger flames in my chest.

I drive slowly home. It is ten-thirty in the morning.

Now is a very bad time for me to lose my job. In spite of my large salary, money is tight. My son Andy is flunking out of high school. In desperation, I've enrolled him in an expensive private school. Maybe all the hours I spent at the hospital over the years have taken a toll on my children. Being a single mom, I had no choice, but now I had hopes that the extra attention might help get him motivated. He isn't off to a very good start. He already failed a hole-digging course.

Amanda is pricey these days, too. Trying to detach her from her dependence on the boyfriend, I put her in a well-known modeling school in Toledo. There is a stiff tuition and she needs special outfits for the competitions. Also, it means a trip to the city every week. Amanda is looking fabulous and has so much self-confidence that it's worth it.

Aside from the money, Lydia is the one I worry about. She's a brilliant child who is full of surprises. Now at fourteen, she seems unhappy and distant. There is an unknown problem between us. I don't know how to reach her.

PROMOTION

TWO WEEKS LATER, I'm surprised with a job offer from the personnel director of downtown Saint Jude's Hospital. Turns out an old friend is now their OR supervisor. She recommended me for an instructor position in their floundering school for nurse anesthetists. It seems like a perfect solution and a new challenge. The hospital is in a run-down neighborhood. They'll be glad to have me. I quickly accept.

That first day I can see that the fifty-year-old building has never been renovated, but is freshly painted inside. I'm told that the maintenance workers are magicians keeping the old beds and equipment repaired.

Six anesthesia students have relocated from various parts of the country, thrilled to be included in even as nebulous a school as this one run by Dr. Uberdo. Nurse anesthesia is a hot career with great earning potential, if you can just pass that certification exam. I feel confident that I can help since just a few years ago, I myself scored in the highest percentile, and I am now working on my Master's Degree.

The students are full of gratitude to me. Now they can continue working toward completion of the course. Dr. Uberdo also is happy, as he isn't very interested in teaching. He just wants free anesthesia coverage at Saint Jude's Hospital and hopes I can teach these six how to do it. The stipend he pays each student is only a small fraction of what a certified anesthetist would cost. Barbara and Kelsey are already pretty good, as they started a year ago. But since the previous instructor quit the whole training program has been on hold for several months.

I review the guidelines and requirements set up by the American Association of Nurse Anesthetists, the national certifying organization. After I finalize the curriculum and incorporate extra courses like administration of spinal anesthesia and chest x-ray interpretation, the Saint Jude's Hospital School of Anesthesia quickly meets and exceeds the requirements. My anesthesia school is accredited and I begin classes.

I give a test every week or two, to keep them studying. I like making up tests but most of all I enjoy the clinical part. In the OR so many things I've learned from my experiences can be shared, subtle important things to keep patients safe and comfortable.

When surgeries for the day are finished one member of the anesthesia team always stays in the hospital overnight, on call for resuscitations and the delivery of babies. Dr. Uberdo comes in from home for emergency surgeries and he and the on-call anesthetist work together.

The on-call room is a former patient room located down the hall from the OR. It's furnished with a scarred bureau, a worn-out stuffed chair upholstered in green Naugahyde, an ancient television without remote control and a hospital bed with the standard plastic-covered mattress and hospital sheets. It is fun to crank up the bed to watch TV, but not fun having to get up to change the channel.

The most pertinent item in the room is the telephone which can summon the anesthetist for an appendectomy, resuscitation, or most likely, the birth of a baby. The on-call anesthetist gets the next day off. Tuesday night is the best night to cover because being off Wednesday breaks up the workweek. Since I make up the schedule I'm always on call Tuesday nights. Second year student Barbara will frequently drop by. The tall Texan woman had moved east to attend the school. Sharp-tongued and quick-witted, she's always good for a laugh but her past is a dark secret. Feeling sad once, she confided to me that she left her children in Texas but doesn't want to talk about it.

Barbara loves all kinds of food. On a Tuesday night she'll often show up unannounced and bang loudly on the call room door. Delighted with herself, she'll present me with a dish, sometimes unidentifiable, that she carefully prepared herself, or procured from some little out of the way ethnic eatery. I'll sit on the side of the bed and she will pull up the old green chair. The odoriferous morsel is set out on the bedside table between us.

One night she brings a whole bag of unpeeled cooked shrimp. Barbara had just come from a local diner where it was "all you can eat" shrimp night. Prior to entering the restaurant she placed a big plastic bag up the wide sleeve of her jacket. She dived into the steaming shrimp and by the time she finished eating, there were about two pounds of hot shrimp up her sleeve.

When I hear the story, with a lop-sided smile I shake my head at the deviousness of my cunning student. But what can I do in the face of such Robin Hood-like generosity? So I just demand, "Well, where's the cocktail sauce?" Our quick reconnaissance of the refrigerator in the OR lounge turns up a half-empty bottle of aged catsup. Barbara has to wrestle it from the sticky shelf.

Heads together, we hunker down over the pile of pink crustaceans on the bedside table. They're still slightly warm. There is silence except for an occasional guttural "mmmm!" It is questionable which smells stronger, the on-call room or Barbara's coat. Some of the shrimp made it into the sleeve but not the plastic bag.

"Ya think the cleaners will be able to get this fish-stink off my coat, Emily?"

"I sure hope so. Watch out. There's a lot of hungry cats in this neighborhood, Barb."

We also share our love of philosophical books and one evening Barbara arrives with a large blue volume under her arm. "I just couldn't get into it."

Page 1 fascinates me. It begins: THIS IS A REQUIRED COURSE. ONLY THE TIME YOU TAKE IT IS UP TO YOU.

"Thanks, Barb. I think I'm gonna like this one. I'm always trying to figure out why things are so messed up. Why do people have to get sick and have pain? Why do they have to have parts of their bodies chopped off? Why do I have to be lonely? I've been trying to figure this stuff out for a long time."

"I don't worry about it, Gal. Eat, drink, and be merry for tomorrow we die, that's what I think."

"I just hate suffering, that's all. I'm really not into suffering."

"Oh well, I'll be the one suffering tomorrow, Em. I got all those cases while you have the day off." Barbara's shoulders slump at the thought.

"I might even get to enjoy my day off if there aren't too many babies born tonight. Get outta here, Barb. I gotta get a little sleep before somethin' starts happening around here." I head for the bathroom with my toothbrush as Barbara shuffles out the door.

"Thanks for the book." I call over my shoulder.

I do like the book. It seems to have some answers. And it gradually convinces me to meditate. When I'm home in the evening and the children are settled in their rooms I begin to sit on the floor in my darkened room, peaceful and alone, attempting to quiet my mind.

Sitting like that one night, something happens. A Voice speaks to me. I can't be sure where it originates. Somehow it seems to come from inside me but not from my own mind. Strangely I'm not concerned. What I actually feel is annoyed, because of what the Voice tells me to do.

"Put your arms up in the air."

When I ignore it the words are spoken again, softly but firmly.

"Put your arms up in the air."

I respond mentally, "No! It's too embarrassing!"

A third time the Voice calmly requests, "Put your arms up in the air."

"Oh all right! I'll do it, just to get you to shut up!"

In the dark, I sheepishly move my arms up. Instantly I am embracing a brilliant beam of light that flows from somewhere above. The blazing light is warm, alive and intelligent. Love pours into me from the white radiance. Indescribable love and comfort and protection flow over me. As I hold on to the beam of light, it sways me gently back and forth like a mother rocking her baby. The light is flowing into my own chest! Tears stream down my face. A powerful feeling of complete happiness fills me up. Bliss, Bliss, Nothing but Bliss.

After a while, I don't know how long, the room is dark again.

How could such a thing happen? I can't accept it. I must be having some kind of a breakdown.

I push the Voice and the Light far from my mind.

THE STUDENTS 13

KELSEY IS THE only anesthetist who doesn't take call in the call room. He can dash across the street from his second-floor apartment in a dilapidated building. Routinely he invites me over for dinner when I'm on call. He likes to cook and I appreciate getting a change of scenery for a couple of hours. I pitch in with some of the meal preparation and cleanup.

Our department doesn't have beepers yet, so I give the hospital operator Kelsey's number so I can be called from there.

The apartment is a neighborhood hub for a covey of Kelsey's male friends, lovers and friends who used to be lovers. When I begin to hang out there, the boys work hard to act straight, but one evening, in the heat of a conversation, they forget. They soon realize that they are out of the closet, so to speak. I don't react, and I've been accepted as one of the gang ever since.

When Kelsey's friend Sammie has his circumcision surgery, he stays at Kelsey's for recuperation. That Tuesday I receive a call to bring over an ice bag. When I arrive, Sammie can be heard moaning and whimpering in the bedroom. The rest of the boys are standing in the living room commiserating, "What is the matter?"

"Is it supposed to hurt like this?"

"Has something gone horribly wrong down there?"

One by one they tiptoe into the bedroom to check poor Sammie's throbbing organ. The ice bag is applied, removed, applied again. Finally Kelsey pleads with the only "expert" present, me.

"Please. Won't you take a look? After all, you've given anesthesia for lots of circumcisions, Emily."

Reluctantly I knock on the door. Taking the high-pitched whine for an invitation, I step into the fetid room. Eyes down, Sammie gingerly lifts the sweaty sheets up.

He has an erection.

"Sammie, no wonder the thing hurts. You must think pure thoughts," I scold.

My hand flies out and my index finger smartly flicks the engorged appendage.

"OOOOOOWWWWWW!"

Instantly five pairs of bulging eyes peer into the room. All are witness to the rapid wilting of the penis followed by a sigh of relief from the patient.

Turning toward the door with a scowl, I bark, "He's fine."

Dr. Uberdo invites the whole department to his home for a swim party. It's a warm, sunny Saturday afternoon. His home is in an upscale development on the outskirts of town. There is a kidney-shaped pool out back surrounded by a white picket fence. His plumpish little wife Maria bustles around in her black sleeveless top and designer Capri pants, serving a platter of miniature hot dogs wrapped in doughy little crusts. The doctor, dressed festively in a red print tropical shirt and shorts proudly shows off his living room. It has a contemporary style, all sharp corners, chrome and geometric designs. In one corner of the room stands a gigantic silver floor lamp shaped like a laryngoscope blade.

Kelsey looks crisp in blue seersucker slacks and starched white dress shirt open at the neck, sleeves rolled up. He helps Dr. Uberdo get everyone started with drinks. In his wrinkled denim shorts Jerry's unruly dark hair and slurpy grin indicate that his partying began earlier. I come in carrying a chocolate cake. My camera is slung around my neck, tangled in my long hair. My tight-fitting red shorts and striped halter top stop the action for an instant as all eyes glance my way. It's amazing how much more attractive we are when not wearing OR scrubs.

We drift out the back door to the pool and find Barbara already horizontal in one of the lounge chairs. She's looking over her shoulder and laughing out loud. As our eyes follow hers, two shadowy figures are silhouetted on the other side of the gate. William's head is bobbing up and down and he's pressing against someone whose white clad rear-end bulges through the gate slats. The gate barely supports their weight as they kiss and embrace. They're oblivious to the hoots and catcalls coming from us.

Another deep-throated cackle sounds from behind the couple. Six-foot-three Rupert has arrived. Sheryl screeches and stumbles backward as the gate suddenly flies open and all three of them burst in, William and Sheryl still wrapped in each other's arms.

Soon after William became a student at Saint Jude's School of Anesthesia, he and Sheryl began dating. Now they are inseparable. He came from the Midwest and always sounds like he's chewing on a piece of straw, but actually there's usually a cigarette in the corner of his mouth. Sheryl is a Toledo gal who comes from a big Irish family. She put herself through nursing school and chose the operating room as her specialty. She is an experienced OR nurse and a valuable member of the team.

Rupert strides past them right up to Dr. Uberdo. Stiffly they shake hands. Rupert comes from far away. His country needs someone to learn the particular skills he's pursuing at Saint Jude's. When he graduates he will go back to Ghana and rejoin his wife and little boy. Meanwhile the big dark skinned fellow is getting a different education from William, Sheryl, Barbara and Kelsey.

As drinks flow and the sun begins to set, the burgers are grilled and devoured. Nonchalantly, Sheryl slips out of her slacks and lacy blouse to reveal a tiny yellow bikini that maximizes her robust figure.

After dipping her toes to test the water she dives headfirst into the deep end.

"The water's warm! Come on in!" she squeals. William sits on the pool's edge, long legs lazily kicking the water toward her. He takes a long drag on his cigarette. Sheryl grabs both his legs and suddenly William is thrashing in the pool and completely submerges as she lunges on top of him.

He pops up sputtering. "Look what you did to my cigarette, you she-cat!" Beaming, he flicks the limp butt onto the deck and pursues her. She shrieks lustily and the water comes alive as they move together and apart, circling and turning in a sensual chase.

I head for the bathroom to put on my bathing suit. It is located in the center of the first floor, with no windows. Too late I close the door and see the weird design. The walls and ceiling are swathed with dramatic swirling bands of crimson and black, with silver mirrored patterns interspersed. Muted lighting coming from little pinholes in the ceiling adds to the psychedelic effect. Maybe those few drinks I had aren't helping. And knowing Dr. Uberdo as well as I do, my paranoia kicks in. Could the walls' silver patches actually be one-way mirrors?

Someone could be out there watching me right now. I put my face up close to the wall.

Can't see out. Hmm. I check another wall. My bladder is expanded way beyond my comfort level.

"I know you're there! You can't fool me, you sicko!" I snarl under my breath. I back slowly around the room, glaring at each wall in turn, sputtering, "I see you, you creep!"

In desperation I quickly relieve myself and hunching over, I slip modestly into my bathing suit. I try to see my reflection on the patterned walls. Wow, this blue bikini sure looks freaky.

"Now let's see. Where's the door? Every wall looks exactly the same! How do I get out of here? Aren't there any brighter lights?" I sweep my hands over the designs but there are no switches on the walls.

"Smells like a funeral home."

Claustrophobia makes me sweat. I run my hands over the walls again in a panic checking for the doorknob.

"I know the door isn't behind the toilet. How 'bout this wall over here? What a horrible creepy place! I hope you're satisfied, you weirdo." Anger sobers me. Now I check the walls more methodically.

"Oh, thank God! Here's a latch!"

I stagger out of the bathroom.

I need another drink. What an experience! But first I prowl around the outside walls of the bathroom. As far as I can tell, there are no one-way mirrors.

The backyard party is in full swing. The night chimes with laughter. There are streams of X-rated retorts and raucous guffaws. Barbara, still in her knit jumpsuit, prances around the edge of the pool, her high-heeled sandals gingerly stepping over wet lumps of discarded swimsuits. Naked Sheryl lumbers up the pool ladder, her ample unsupported breasts swaying from side to side. She bounds around the deck and it just takes a little shove. Barbara is propelled, screaming, into the pool, her black pants ballooning out around her. A spotlight on the roof silhouettes Sheryl's broad gluteus muscles and sparkles the little diamond droplets all over her pink flesh. Hands on her hips, she hollers, "You can drink more booze if you swim, Babs!"

Rupert's teeth blaze against his ebony skin. He's treading water in the deep end and must be thinking how much Sheryl's naked-ness reminds him of his homeland and his own family. Still, he isn't inclined to remove his own swimsuit. Dr. Uberdo surreptitiously watches the pool scene as he sits chatting with Kelsey and Jerry in another corner of the yard. There's a sneer on his face. I wonder how much his wife is observing. She disappeared into the house as soon as the food was served.

After a quick dip in the pool I decide to maintain my decorum as instructor and not subject myself to the boisterous pool antics. The sudden removal of my bikini by one of my students is a distinct possibility if I hang around long enough.

I say my goodbyes and head for home still wearing my wet suit. I am absolutely not using that bathroom again.

I arrive at Kelsey's one Tuesday evening to find Sheryl sitting sideways on the couch folding laundry. Heaped on the floor around her are ten or twelve bulging green plastic trash bags. As we chat about various recent events in the OR I'm thinking about how I admire Sheryl and the way she always remains cool no matter what the situation, and how nothing is ever too much trouble. She is a hard worker.

Sheryl's folded piles grow higher and higher. I wonder if all the full bags could possibly be holding more laundry.

"Where'd you get all that stuff, Sheryl?"

"Oh, I did wash today." She nonchalantly adds another pair of lace panties to a towering mound of other lace panties.

"Where did all this laundry come from?"

"I hate the Laundromat, so I haven't done wash since Christmas."

"But, Sheryl, this is June!"

"Yeah, I know. That's why I have all these bags. When my sheets and towels and clothes get dirty, I just buy more. I have forty-eight sets of sheets and over three hundred pairs of underpants, now all clean!"

"You should be proud of yourself, Sheryl. Whatever motivated you to do wash?"

"Well, Emily, I need to stop shopping so I can save some money. William and I want to go to the beach next month. It's a tough decision but sometimes we have to do hard things."

"Well anyway, I'll know where I can borrow a sheet or something." I smirk.

THE GENTLE MAN

"THERE'S A DATING service I just heard about, Emily. Maybe you oughta check it out." Michelle and I are sitting in our usual booth at the luncheonette.

"Gee, why would I want to get involved in something like that?" Then my curiosity kicks in. "What do you know about it?"

"Well, I heard one of the nurses talking about it. She said she met a nice guy. Anyway, here's how it works. They come out to your place and interview you and find out about your hobbies and interests. You can tell them what you like and don't like. For instance, if you want to meet someone of a certain religion. You also can give them the name of any creep you don't want to meet. The service sends you a photo of every guy they match you with and a card with their info. Then if he calls, you already have a clue what he might be like. I think you should give it a try, just for the fun of it."

I have to admit I'm intrigued. "Did ya get the number?"

Michelle scrunches her face up as she rifles through her voluminous leather bag. Eventually she pulls out a tattered yellow scrap of paper. "Aha! I found it!"

Soon I'm getting referrals. Some show up looking ten or fifteen years older or fifty pounds heavier than their photo. It makes me wonder what else they might be fibbing about. After dating a few guys, I learn that they always want at least a big smooch at the end of the date. After dealing with surgeons all day I'm in no mood to be lovey-dovey with someone I just met. They quickly get the message that this stone-faced woman is going to be trouble. They make a speedy exit and I never hear from them again.

Then Matthew calls. I laugh at his photo because it shows his obvious distaste in posing for the picture that will be sent out to strangers. I had that same reaction when my interviewer whipped out the camera. Matt is soft spoken with a minor southern accent. Our first conversation feels comfortable and we talk again a few days later. Matt is also divorced. Even though I have three teenage children, he seems interested. He has two of his own, who live with their mother. I usually don't bother with newspapers or keep informed about world events, but the night before our first date, it's quiet at work and I read a news magazine I find in the call room.

When I meet Matt for dinner, I can't help but smile. He actually looks better than his photo. Here is an honest guy, and good-looking, too. Five years older than me, his hair is thinning on top. His skin glows like a really clean person who doesn't smoke or overindulge. I'm immediately attracted. That feels good too. When we finally say goodnight he doesn't touch me. He doesn't move in for his "payment." We just look into each other's eyes (his are crystalline blue) and smile.

What a relief. A real gentleman! I hope he'll call again.

And he does. Months later, Matt confides that one of the first things that impressed him about me was how well-informed I was about world events.

"Matt and I are talking about moving in together, Michelle. What do you think about that?" We're sitting at the central island in Michelle's modern kitchen, having coffee.

"I am so happy that you are finally having impure thoughts! You're growing beyond the Catholic way of thinking. The two of you are consenting adults, so why not? You better be sure he's 'The One' though. It will be tough on the kids if they get attached to him and then he's gone."

"Yeah, they already had that happen with their dad. But I'm sure, all right. He is the most satisfying man in all ways."

"You look radiant, Emily."

"Aw, it's just the glow of your rosy kitchen walls, Michelle."

"Well please, spare me the gory details. I hate hearing about all that passion and stuff."

"What's the matter, Michelle? You didn't mind listening to all the grief and suffering. Why can't you enjoy hearing about the happy stuff?"

"Because it isn't happening to me, you dummy. My guy falls asleep at nine. He's a low-energy man, unfortunately for me." Squirming on her rose bar stool, my friend puckers her brow.

"Can't ya slip him some B12 or somethin?"

"Can we please not discuss this?"

"Sorry, gal. But I'm concerned. Will you still be my friend when Matt and I are living in sin?" I flip my curly hair.

"You better believe it. You're my role model, Em. I'm so proud of you! When we first became friends you were living in poverty, with the electric company shutting off your power. And Paul was slapping you around. You looked ten years older, all haggard and depressed." Michelle's head slowly moves from side to side. "I can't imagine how hard it must have been for you to go back to school for anesthesia training. But you stuck to it and now you are providing a nice life for your children, all by yourself."

I take a long swallow of coffee.

"You don't know the half of it, Michelle. Learning to give anes-thesia was the hardest thing I ever did. For the first nine months my heart rate never went below one hundred. I stank from sweat-ing in fear all the time. I used to run into the ladies room and do deep breathing exercises and self-hypnosis. RELAX! RELAX! I'd tell myself. But by the end of my training I was competent. I was in control, and I was making lots of money. With my first paycheck, the kids and I drove to the local TV store, plunked down cash and pointed to their biggest color set. They loaded it into the trunk of my old car. It barely fit. All we had up till then was a little twelve inch black and white TV.

"Of course five days a week, I drove an hour into the worst neighborhood in the city to that rundown little hospital on Seventh Street. I was the only nurse anesthetist there. One anesthesiologist and I ran the two ORs."

I help myself to a mouthful of Danish.

"I don't know how you got the nerve, Emily. Weren't you afraid of getting mugged or raped or something?"

"For what they paid me, it would have been worth it. But the people there treated me like God. When I'd park my car on the street behind the hospital, some old guy sitting on his front porch across the street would keep an eye on it all day. Leaving the hospital one day I found I had a flat tire. I had run over a nail. Three kids who were playing basketball in the street changed the tire for me, just like that. I tried to pay them, but they wouldn't take any money. One of them told me, 'You took good care of my grandma and now the kids from Kennytown get a chance to help you.'"

Changing the subject, Michelle raises her eyebrows. "Well, Emily, Matt has a lot to measure up to. But from what you've told me, he's real solid with a good career. So go for it! You deserve all the love and joy you can get."

"You are a great friend, Michelle. My family will have a fit, but where were they when I needed them the most? Dad didn't speak to me for a month when Paul and I split up. I had burst the bubble of his perfect family. They'll just have to get used to it. I intend to remain free. No more legal tangles."

"After what you had to pay for your divorce from Paul, I don't blame you, Em. Why not keep it simple."

We've had a death in the family. A car hit our dog Sparky last week, right in front of the house. She loved to run, and you couldn't stop her when she got loose. Totally fearless, she liked to chase cars. This time she lost the race big-time. The kids and I were pretty upset. Then my sister Sally said she was having allergy problems and was looking for a home for her new dog. His name is Mr. Boy, and he looks almost identical to our mutt Sparky. They both have the golden fur like a retriever but smaller in size. It is comforting to have him here. He's very affectionate and is making it easier for us to get over our loss of poor Sparky.

One afternoon Paul just shows up, shirtless and in shorts. I see him playing with the kids in the backyard while I'm working on supper. Suddenly he lets out a terrific howl. The kids are laughing as I run outside. What a spectacle. Mr. Boy is hanging on to Paul's bare belly by his teeth.

"Come here, Mr. Boy! It's okay. Let him loose." My shout causes the dog to release him. Secretly I am applauding the protective dog.

"Now that you've been 'formally' introduced, say hello to Mr. Boy, Paul. This is not Sparky, and he doesn't know who you are. He is guarding the children!" I try to hide my smirk. This is my kind of dog.

When Matt gets home from work, I introduce him to the guy I've been complaining about for so long. Of course Paul the "intellectual" immediately sets out to make Matt look like a dummy. Over dinner he questions Matt about his hobbies.

"I like to read." Matt tells him as he plays along with the interrogation. He is unaware that Paul reads very esoteric literature. You might say he is a literary snob.

"What do you read?" Paul keenly sets the bait. He will demonstrate to me how much smarter he is than this new guy in my life.

"Oh, I read Reader's Digest."

Matt's answer stuns him. Paul is speechless. It's much worse than he thought. Our eyes meet, and he sees mirth sparkling in mine. I can tell he is in a quandary. Was this a setup? How can I care for this man who doesn't surf? Matt probably couldn't fix a car either. What Paul doesn't know is that Matt was an officer in the navy, has a steady job, and doesn't need to fix his own car. I serve the chocolate cake. Paul is silent.

There is one thing they do have in common: cancer. Matt's company begins to provide complete physical exams for all the managers. It includes a sigmoidoscopy. After the exam, Matt tells me a suspicious polyp was found. I struggle to not react, but everything inside me knots up in a cold ball. I instinctively know Matt has cancer. A week later he freaks out when he gets the biopsy report.

"I have colon cancer. I'm only forty-eight! How can this be happening to me?"

I've had a whole week to steel myself for the bad news, and can be calm.

"We'll go see Dr. Shillinger. He'll fix it for you."

Luckily, the low anterior resection does not require a colostomy. After the surgery, Matt has chemotherapy for a year and a half. He gets a shot every morning on his way to work. This is a turning point in our relationship. Up until now we've focused on our five children. Suddenly we don't know how much time we have left. Every moment becomes even sweeter and more intense.

THE ASHRAM 15

MY FATHER CAN'T accept the fact that his oldest daughter's marriage is over. The Irishman's greatest pride was always his large Catholic family. Why isn't his daughter more subservient? Other women just put up with stuff. Marriage is supposed to be forever, isn't it? Even worse, I am now living in sin, just like his despicable mother-in-law (my beloved grandmother) did years ago.

Then my brother Jason goes through a painful divorce. The two of us feel like the black sheep of the family. And Jason has apparently gotten involved in a cult. As his older sister I need to look out for him, so I agree to visit him at the ashram. I almost don't go. The night before, I'm having second thoughts. Why should I drive all that way south east into the mountains, four hours away? From deep inside me I hear these words: "YOU CAN'T GROW IN A VACUUM."

What inner being is advising me? Okay, then. I will go.

Expecting a bunch of old rundown shacks and an outhouse, I'm surprised to see well-tended gardens and comfortable chairs in the lobby. My brother looks happier than I've ever seen him. The people he introduces me to are well dressed and self-confident, not hippie-like at all.

We talk for hours about life. For the first time in ages I feel encouraged about my own chance for happiness.

When I mention "cult" he tells me, "A cult is when they want you to be dependent on them and they want your money. Everyone here is free to stay or leave. This spiritual path is not interested in your money. Room rent here is twenty-five dollars and includes great vegetarian meals. Of course, you may have a few roommates."

Yes, there are four sets of bunk beds and only one bathroom. I shudder at the thought of eight women sharing one bathroom. . But it beats the weather-beaten shack with an outhouse I was expecting.

Jason brings up the spiritual framework in which we grew up. "You and I were already in a religion that wanted us to be dependent on it. Remember going to Hell if you ever ate meat on Friday or missed Mass on Sunday? Remember going to confession?"

I ask him, "But, why would I ever need a meditation master?"

My brother responds, "If you wanted to learn how to play golf wouldn't you get yourself the best teacher? The same is true for learning meditation."

In the evening everyone gathers in an expansive hall. The teacher swaggers in and strides down the center aisle. He wears a bright white long silk garment and, even though it's July, a blue knit hat, the kind our mom makes. He sits in front on a wide chair, his legs pretzeled under him. He is rotund but not jolly. He comes from India but he reminds me of my father. It's the way he carries himself, relaxed and very much in control. I start to tune him out when he begins to speak. Gee, he doesn't even speak English.

But I become totally captivated by the translator. The words flow through this radiant woman to the crowd in a seamless river. It seems as though the words are speaking deeply to me. The room fades away as I listen raptly.

Later Jason and I join a slow snaking line toward the chair where the teacher is chatting with people. I'm glad I wore the gauzy white outfit with the long shirt. My brother seems delighted that I fit in so well. "You can ask him a question if you want," he tells me.

I think about young Andy threatening to quit school and Amanda with another new boyfriend. Why is Lydia always so sullen and noncommunicative? When we come to the teacher, I ask him, "How can I help my children find peace?"

He responds, "Love them and always wish them well." He pauses, and then continues, "Bring them here for seven days. That will teach them self-discipline."

When I get to my room I'm glad no one else is there. I need to be alone. I'm having two opposite reactions simultaneously. My mind is in turmoil. And I feel joyous. Logically I don't even like that guru. But ecstatic tears are pouring down my cheeks. Oh no! Am I sobbing out loud?

What is this happiness I'm feeling? I must be having a breakdown. I was afraid this would eventually happen, just like my mother. I remember back in second grade and Mom was in a mental hospital. I was so embarrassed at school because the nun made all the kids pray for her.

Now it must be happening to me. I haven't cried for a long time. I feel as though my heart is bursting open and all this overwhelming joy is gushing out of me. This can't be good. I have to keep it a secret as long as I can.

I never confided in any of my siblings and I'm not starting now. Jason won't find out from me about my breakdown. He's talked me into signing up for a special two-day meditation program. Maybe this probably boring program will stabilize my condition.

For two days, I sit in the big room with several hundred other poor souls. As always, my mind works over-time. This teacher is such a charlatan. I can see trick blue lighting around him and the translator. And this electricity I feel shooting across my chest! Obviously they have the place wired!

My irritation grows into anger, and then into intense rage. All the anger against my parents and my abusive husband builds into an inferno inside me. During the meditation, I remember the time I slammed Paul in the face with a full platter of turkey, potatoes and gravy. In my mind's eye I again see hot lumps of mashed potatoes sliding down our dining room wall and gravy dripping off his nose. I don't remember why I did it, but I know he deserved it.

The meditation master gives a talk. And he goes on and on. His timer sounds off. It is reset, only to repeat the process until they finally stop setting it. Everyone around me is squirming and fidgeting. Except I see one little man who is grinning widely and nodding in agreement with whatever is said. Hmmm. That raises my interest, and I start really listening.

I hear him saying, "You are the sky. You are the trees. You are the sun. You are the leaves. You are the ocean. You are the moon."

He names practically everything in the universe. At last it ends and I am truly sorry it is over. I wander out into the sunlight. Everything feels different. I can't explain it, but I am the grass. I am the sky.

Still, after two days, I carry a tremendous sizzling ball of rage down the same snaking line to the teacher. My face would stop a clock. Our eyes finally meet and he glares at me! I feel a twinge of fear. I have a fleeting concern that he'll put a curse on me.

A loud HAHAHA erupts from the guru's translator, her dark eyes flitting from the master's scowl to my scowl as she sees him mirroring me.

I guess it's okay if the translator is laughing.

Driving home for hours that night, a violent storm crashes around me. Lightning flashes and torrential rain floods the road. Massive tractor trailer trucks roar past, honking and splashing waves across my windshield. In the dark, terrified and ecstatic, I loudly chant the mantra and sob all the way home.

The phone rings. It's Jason. "Well, Emily, what did you think about the ashram?"

"I have to admit, it is a peaceful place. And the food is pretty good, except for that weird cereal. Too much pepper! What are they thinking? Anyway, I just don't know about the meditation master. What is the point of having one? Why would I, Emily, need such a person in my life?"

He chuckles. "Remember the chant we did early every morning?"

"Boy, do I remember it. It went on and on. After a while I looked through the chanting book to see how much more was left. What a shock. That chant has pages and pages of verses, all in Sanskrit. I'm still amazed that I sat through the whole thing." I won't admit that I felt unusually at peace when it was over. I wanted that feeling to go on and on.

I can sense Jason's glee over the phone. "To answer your question, if you want to know what the master is good for, just do that chant every day."

"Oh I don't think so, Jason."

Still, when I was in the hall listening to the relentless chant, I was impressed that everyone else was chanting away. The strange language flowed off their tongues as if they could speak it fluently. That challenges me. Maybe it wouldn't be a bad idea. At least if I ever go back, I'd like to be able to rattle it off like they do. I sure can't meditate with this active mind of mine. I can't even get a good night's sleep most of the time. But I remember that one of the monks made an interesting statement. He said, "Chanting quiets the mind, and after chanting for a time, a person will be able to meditate."

Thus begins my spiritual practice of chanting. Every morning before dawn I sit cross-legged in my little meditation room with an audio tape and my chanting book. Through this practice, over the years, each verse has come alive, sharing its secrets, layer upon layer. I've come to know the saints in verse fifty-two. One Christmas morning, during my chant I mentally invite them to come for our big turkey dinner that night.

Later that afternoon, when the turkey had been in the oven for hours, there's a knock at the door. A workman stands outside in the snow and tells us there is a leak in the gas main in our street. They have to shut off the gas. I tell him our turkey isn't quite done and he asks how much time I need.

"Another forty-five minutes should do it." "Okay, he says. "We'll wait."

When the turkey is cooked I go out and give them the go-ahead. And I ask, "Why don't you join us for dinner?" Their faces light up. The head of the crew says maybe, after they finish the repair work.

I tell them, "Sure! Just bang on our door when you are ready. We'll be happy to have you."

When our family is just finished dessert, six burly men in their work boots tromp into the kitchen. They wash up and dive into a vast spread of turkey and all the fixings, chowing down with gusto. One of them shares with me that he had been planning to eat a couple of hot dogs when he got to his own place. It is dark by the time they finish their pumpkin pie. They head out into the frigid night to deal with another emergency.

By 11:00 p.m. my kitchen has been put back together again and my family has settled into their rooms. Matt and I are finally relaxing in the living room. A knock comes at the front door. When I open it there stands one of the workmen. He presents me with a bouquet of fresh flowers.

"For the cook," he announces with a big grin, his breath making steam in the cold air.

Where did he ever find flowers at eleven o'clock Christmas night? My heart aches for the joy of it. My Saints came to dinner!

I met the teacher in 1979, but it wasn't until 1983 that I noticed that my violent temper was gone! Giving him my anger, I didn't realize that it was for all time. Oh sure, I can get pissed off, but now it's just like a little cloud passing over, not the explosions of my past. What an amazing gift has been given to me! My heart is full of gratitude.

With regards to the apparent "trick lighting" I perceived on my first visit to the ashram, none existed. I was actually seeing a powerful blue aura around the master and his translator.

TWO PATIENTS

MICHELLE STILL WORKS at Robertsboro Hospital and often has news. After one of our gym workouts she whispers, "Emily, come sit in my car. I have something confidential to tell you."

Gosh, this must be serious. We quickly climb into the front seat of Michelle's Corvair and face each other. I curl my legs up under me.

"The other night there was a woman in labor. It was her sixth child. She had given birth five times without a problem, but this baby just wouldn't come out. Her obstetrician kept yelling at her to push. Dr. Panute was on duty for anesthesia, and he was giving her some gas to help things along. After a while Panute got impatient and hollered to the obstetrician, 'I'll help you, Doc!' Jumping up on a footstool for leverage, he started pressing on her belly. He's real strong ya know. But the baby was really stuck. Then he gave a powerful thrust and her belly gave way."

My eyes widen in disbelief. I take a deep breath and picture the delivery room scene. I've witnessed staff members pressing on a woman's belly, but nothing bad ever happened.

"The woman's scream was horrible. The whole shape of her abdomen changed, sort of went flat. Then her blood pressure dropped. They rushed her to the OR and knocked her out. The surgeons found her uterus and bladder were ruptured. They had popped like two balloons. The baby was floating among the blood, intestines, urine and amniotic fluid. He was dead. He weighed ten pounds, a lot bigger than her other kids."

"What the woman needed was a C Section! What happened to her?" I shift my position.

"Last I heard, she's still alive in the Intensive Care Unit."

"Wow! And we're supposed to 'do no harm.' That rotten Panute made a big mistake this time. What do you think will happen?"

"Oh, Em, you know how these doctors protect each other. Even though the obstetrician is distraught about what happened, he'll never report it. It's already all hushed up. I heard about this from my friend who was on duty that night."

At Saint Jude's I'm running the cystoscopy room, a cramped little space with a special cysto table. There's a drain in the floor for these urologists who are always splashing water around. My curly hair is tucked into a green OR cap that coordinates with the color of my eyes. On purpose, the clogs add to my height. I have two anesthesia students in tow. Jerry and William hover around the anesthesia cart where I've placed labeled syringes containing my choice of drugs for this particular patient.

A man in his sixties is wheeled into the room on a stretcher. Mouth pinched, his eyes dart around apprehensively. His sparse salt and pepper hair is uncombed; the loose hospital gown drooping down exposes a hairy chest. He smells like a two-pack-a-dayer, and the stained fingertips prove it. I look him in the eye, smile and introduce the team. The boys glance up and nod. They're slumped over the chart reviewing the permit, labs and other parameters they've learned to check as part of the anesthetist's disciplined routine. As we chat, he visibly relaxes and when the surgeon walks in, the man seems ready to surrender himself to the process.

Meanwhile, across the hall in his office, Anesthesia chief Dr. Uberdo is doing what he does every day. He picks at his calculator, adding up the anesthesia payments that came in today's mail. I imagine he is scheming how to spend the money. As the day wears on he takes several phone calls and continues to work the numbers.

Finally the surgeries are finished, and the boys clean the equipment. I check in with Chief Uberdo.

"Oh, by the way," he hems and haws, "somebody in ICU needs to be intubated and placed on a ventilator. They've been calling all day about it." Head bowed, he won't make eye contact with me.

"She has that Legionnaires Disease. She could be real contagious. We don't even know."

Grabbing my emergency box I run for the stairs. That little coward. He doesn't want to expose himself so he waits until someone else is available.

The ICU nurse is upset and vocal. She snarls at me, "Even though she's under infectious disease precautions, we still need to take care of her! We've been calling for anesthesia service for hours! She's ready to have a cardiac arrest! You better hurry up!"

The patient's strident gasp can be heard from the doorway. I hastily don a gown, mask and gloves and approach the bed. My hand on the ashen-faced woman's wrist informs me of a pulse that is weak and irregular. Yes, she will "code" soon.

"Margaret, I'm going to put a breathing tube down your throat so you can breathe better," I calmly inform the patient. Margaret is concerned only with her next breath. She is exhausted trying to pull air into her fluid-filled chest. Her strength is all used up. The tube goes in smoothly. As soon as the ventilator is hooked up Margaret's heart begins beating stronger and steadier as 100 percent oxygen is forced into her drowning lungs. The tension in the room eases. My work is done.

Two weeks later while making rounds I run into the same ICU nurse. She is wheeling a perky white haired woman toward the door for discharge.

"Margaret wants to say something to you, Emily."

Our eyes meet. She holds my hand for a long moment.

"Thank you." The woman's eyes shine with tears.

KARMA

I HASTILY STRAIGHTEN up the living room. Michelle is coming over with some big news. I wonder what she could be so excited about. As soon as my friend bursts through the door she grabs my arm.

"You gotta be sittin' down for this one, girlfriend!"

"Don't you even want a cup of coffee first?"

"Just hear me out, Emily. You won't believe this."

I park myself on the couch while Michelle drags a stuffed chair up close so we sit facing each other.

Dramatically Michelle sets the scene. "It all started in the endoscopy suite. Your friend Dr. Panute was covering that room, only because somebody called in sick. Naturally he was in a mean mood, and the nurses were already frustrated. The first patient was so rammy they couldn't even get his IV started. The guy just stood there rocking back and forth on his heels. His orderlies were holding on to him, but when anyone else came close he would start yellin' and try to swing at them."

Michelle kicks off her shoes and continues.

"A friend of mine was working in the room. She said Panute checked the chart real quick to see if he could cancel the case."

Michelle imitates Panute's strident tone of voice. "Fifty-two years old, has mental capacity of a two-year-old. Rectal bleeding. Guess we gotta do it. Didn't get his Haldol. No wonder he's goin' nuts. But so what! I'm a lot bigger than this retard. We'll just muscle 'im down and I'll hit 'im with the ole Ketamine in the butt. That's some good shit. Even with a whoppin' big dose they keep breathin'. You could skin 'em alive an' they wouldn't even know it. See how he likes that! He'll be sweet as pie in no time."

I hoot and flap my arms. "Your Panute production is perfect! Go on!"

"My friend couldn't believe how Panute was ranting. Then he calmed down a little and started bragging to Dr. Feldman, the surgeon. Panute told him how it felt good to get his adrenalin pumping, 'cause some babe wore him out last night."

Michelle parodied Panute's jargon. "She looked real cute from across the bar, but up close and personal she was kinda rough. After a night like that, I was looking forward to a relaxing day here. When I signed up for Anesthesia Chief, who knew I'd be standin' around drinkin' coffee 'n' watchin' chitlins on a TV screen all day. But with Navana out sick, I gotta run a room, and this'll be the easiest one."

I shriek at Michelle's performance.

"You look just like him. You got the mannerisms down too. I can just picture his cocky expression." Then I scrunch up my face in disgust and comment, "What an arrogant bastard. Imagine talking like that to old Dr. Feldman. Panute is such a total scum. Go on, Michelle."

"Then Panute snapped at the nurses." Michelle jumps up and starts imitating the anesthesiologist in his high-pitched voice, "Come on! Never mind the IV. Have those goons walk him right into the endo room here. I'll shut him up. I've had these retarded guys plenty of times before. The nitwit nurses at the Home don't give 'im his tranquilizers 'cause his stomach has to be empty for the colonoscopy. Then we gotta deal with this wild man."

I can't stop laughing. I have to admit, those patients are definitely a challenge. I can almost empathize.

"Well, the orderlies started walking the guy into the endo room, with Panute bossing them around at the top of his lungs, which didn't reassure the patient any."

She slides into her Panute routine again. "Get control of him, boys! Sling 'im face down on that stretcher now, so I can jab 'im real quick! Watch those legs! Lord, he's strong like a bull. Good thing you guys are bulkers. Hold 'im down, now. Listen to him roar! Here I come. Ya got 'im?"

I jump in. "So now they were holding the poor guy face down on the bed?"

"Yeah. Then Panute grabbed him on the back of his thigh and with the other hand he jammed that needle into the patient's butt, right through his pants. With an awful howl the guy bucked up, causing the needle to bounce out of him and into the back of Panute's hand! Panute rammed it right back into the guy and squirted Ketamine into his buttock."

"Oh my gosh!" I jump up. "You're telling me that the needle stuck the patient, then Panute, then the patient again?"

"You got the picture, gal. And Panute was livid. His hand was bleeding bad. He wiped it with alcohol swabs but the blood was dripping down his wrist. He went over to the sink and ran cold water on his hand."

I slump back on the couch. "What happened to the poor patient?"

"Finally he stopped squirming around. The nurses were all standing around gawking. One of them said, 'He's getting relaxed now, Doctor. Are you okay?'

"He growled a few choice curses. The nurse said, 'Maybe you should go to emergency room and get looked at. Have you had the hepatitis vaccine? This patient has hep B, I believe.'"

I lean forward. "Really? Was that true?"

"Oh yeah, girlfriend. But you ain't heard nothin' yet." Michelle has a smug look.

"Anyway, Panute freaked out. He hadn't seen that on the chart, but sure enough, the guy was a carrier. So he yelled for them to get somebody else to take over and he ran over to the emergency room."

"Do you mean to tell me he just abandoned that patient? If he weren't the boss, he would have been fired for that!"

"Now Em, I told ya. Shut up and let me finish my story!" Michelle grins impishly.

"You mean there's more?"

"Of course! I have friends all over that hospital. I got all the details. So over in the ER he was sweating pretty good. Naturally he wasn't happy about having to go through the whole rigmarole of getting blood drawn to see if he already had hepatitis BEFORE he got stuck with the dirty needle. Of course he never bothered to get the vaccine last year when the rest of us got it. After a while they gave him a bunch of injections in his rear end—gamma globulin and some hepatitis antibodies to hopefully keep him from contracting it."

Michelle takes a deep breath. "So after that he wasn't feeling too good. He stayed home with a sore bottom I guess, and waited for the test results on the blood. They were testing the patient for HIV, too."

"Oh, brother!" My eyes open wider.

"Now wait till you hear this! A few days later the ER called him to come in to get the test results. The nurse who phoned him said he started carrying on over the phone, ranting at her that he can't believe it, he's a damn doctor, for God's sake, and what a bunch of bull this is. But she just told him, 'We never discuss these things over the phone.' Then she hung up on him.

"Speaking of 'hung up,' when he arrived in the ER, he stunk of booze. He drove himself there drunk, Emily!"

"Can you imagine, Michelle? Think of all the people on the road that day!" I shake my head.

Michelle continues, "Yeah, and he just about had smoke coming out of his ears he was so mad when he got there, yelling, 'Who do you think you are, treating the chief of Anesthesia like dirt!'

"So the head nurse dealt with him very professionally. She told him, 'There's good news. You don't have hepatitis A, B or C.'

"His temper tantrum simmered down when he heard that.

"The nurse waited a moment. Then she announced, 'The bad news, however, is—'

"He butted in. 'Bad news? What are you talking about now?'

"He was beginning to sober up fast. She didn't prolong it any more. In a quiet voice she told Panute. 'We will be monitoring the patient you stuck with your dirty needle for HIV now. You are HIV positive. You were already HIV positive when you stuck him, Doctor.'"

My jaw drops open. I am speechless.

But Michelle is still not finished. "Yes, AIDS!

Emily, he's gone. He resigned on the spot. No one has seen him since."

I'm thunderstruck. One word comes to mind: Karma.

A MISTAKE

18

IT IS TUESDAY midnight. The hospital's public address system blasts "CODE 99 PEDIATRICS! CODE 99, PEDIATRICS!" Simultaneously, the phone in the dark anesthesia call-room jangles. Suddenly awake, I grab the receiver and hoarsely shout, "I got it! I got it! Peds, right? I'm on my way!" Sliding my size nines into clogs, I sling my equipment bag over one shoulder, slam the door shut behind me and dash to the children's ward.

The resuscitation is already in progress. A nurse at the foot of the bed quickly gives me a report.

"Twelve-year-old with pneumonia. Looks like nine, he's so tiny. His breathing was okay, then suddenly he started coughing and his color went bad."

At the head of the bed, the other RN scuttles aside and hands me the breathing bag and mask she was pressing onto the boy's blanched face. A defibrillator cart stands near the bed. Its alarm is warning of the straight line on the monitor. The third nurse's chest compressions look tentative. Is she trying not to bruise him? The house physician leading the resuscitation barks, "Better pump a little harder there. We're not getting any perfusion."

I swiftly insert an endotracheal tube down the boy's throat and hook up the breathing bag to it. Reaching behind me I turn the oxygen gauge up higher. The dim lighting eerily plays on the team's desperate movements as we struggle in the heat of the tight cubicle. Dread of a bad outcome hangs over us like a wet blanket.

The sound of sobbing can be heard now. Someone is consoling the child's grandmother out in the hallway, but not allowing her to enter. Finally the disheveled house physician and I share a long look. Then he speaks softly. "It's been twenty five minutes with nothing. No point in continuing."

Reluctantly the team members step away from the lifeless little body until I am alone. I slowly gather my scattered laryngoscope blade and handle. Out of habit, I turn back to cut off the high oxygen flow.

That's when I see it. Motionless I stare at the gauge.

Breath is forced out of me as if a sledgehammer is slammed into my chest.

The lines are crossed. The oxygen line is connected to the suction and the suction line is plugged into the oxygen outlet. No oxygen was administered. We have actually been sucking oxygen out of the boy's lungs.

A sour taste of bile assaults my throat. I try to swallow but have no saliva.

Someone hooked it up wrong and I never noticed it. I never checked it.

My gut twists in a belly cramp. A groan, more like a whimper, escapes me. Moisture trickles down my sides inside my scrub shirt, giving off a whiff of salt and fear.

Beseechingly my fingers brush the boy's curly black hair. The small face is already turning cold.

Then I disconnect everything, square my shoulders and walk out to speak with his granny.

"We did the best we could, ma'am. I'm sorry."

The grief stricken woman holds my clammy hand in hers. "I know you did. I'm praying for you." She shakes her head sadly.

Back in the call room I curl under the blanket, mourning the child who never got his chance to grow up. I lie awake dry-eyed, breathing the words over and over until morning, "I'm sorry, little guy."

The next day I call my brother Jason at the ashram.

"How can I go on in this career? I made a real bad mistake the other night. I don't know whether I killed the little boy, but I sure didn't help him to live."

"Well, Emily, you're a human being and these things can happen. You've saved so many lives and helped people from suffering. Do you think this one incident warrants giving up and not using your special skills anymore? Very few people can do what you do day in and day out. If it's the boy's time, there's nothing you can do to stop his death."

"Well, he didn't have to die on MY shift, did he?" I snort. "Thanks, Bro. It always helps to talk with you."

I decide I will go back to work.

But I must be more vigilant. And I must pray more.

The beach is my solace. I stroll along the water's edge, feet in the wet sand. My mind resting in the moment, I revel in the bay's play, ever seeking to touch me. A wave reaches close, then recedes, only to reach a little further, drawing a new line in the sand each time. Then, with a huge thrust, the water finally swirls the salty foam over my ankles and rolls back into itself again. It makes me laugh to be kissed like that.

Silence. This is the moment when the tide changes, the pause between the in-breath and the out-breath, the in tide and the out tide.

Six of us sit on the beach together, bathed in the early sun, chanting our morning prayer. The crisp fall air smells salty when warmed. The sky is filled with hundreds of monarch butterflies. This orange and yellow rain floats and flutters all around us, flowing from land across the water, migrating south to the sound of the bay and our song.

Matt and I are taking ballroom dancing lessons. We signed up for eight, but have continued for eight years. Matt is fun because he has developed a wonderful lead. I never know what is coming next, but he guides me smoothly around the floor.

We were practicing a Viennese Waltz one evening in Miriam's ballroom with the sprung maple floor. Suddenly the heel of my dance shoe caught on the strap on my other foot, effectively tying my feet together. I was dancing backward in high heels, and Matt kept coming. We went down, him falling on top of me. Somehow he was able to place his fist behind my head to save me. His other hand held most of his weight off me. Amazingly the only injury was a bruise on his fist. We didn't dance the Viennese any more.

The Mummer's Strut, now that is another story! Oh, them Golden Slippers! How we strut our stuff. Some Saturday nights we drive to a huge ballroom, a supermarket transformed into a place to dance. Quickly we learn we can't drink and do our fancy steps. Just as well. We don't need that anyway.

I joined a barbershop chorus. We sing four part harmony. After my brother's wife Laura joined we livened up the group by writing shows. We'd take the chorus's repertoire and create a story using those songs.

It seems that practicing chanting and meditation has freed me from all fear and self-consciousness. Oh, the bliss of dancing and singing!

THE LETTER

19

ONE EVENING, ON call and bored, I explore all the little unused nooks and hidden places in Saint Jude's antiquated operating room suite and find something very interesting. Right next to Dr. Uberdo's office, there is a closet-like room. Inside, on one of the dusty shelves is a large metal box. It looks like a safe, ancient and rusted. A tattered and faded note is taped to it. Although barely legible, I can see that it is a warning. "This Container is Leaking Radiation. Danger to All Within 50 Feet."

This radio-active container is right against the wall of Dr. Uberdo's office. Sitting at his desk every day, he is within ten feet of the radiation!

The next day I show him what I found. As usual, he just brushes me off. He's in a state of total denial that there could be any problem. He probably won't do anything about it. Then I remember he mentioned that he and his wife were trying to have a baby. The devil in me comes out as I cajole him.

"I wonder if all that radiation is frying your most important parts, Doctor," I say with a smirk.

Two days later, two people wearing special protective garments come and haul the box away.

The neighborhood women all have their babies delivered here at our hospital. The anesthesia department is usually called upon to provide analgesia for the deliveries. An antiquated Brand X anesthesia machine is turned on and a mask placed over the nose and mouth of the mother-to-be. A 50 percent oxygen and 50 percent nitrous oxide mixture is considered safe and provides some pain relief, but won't make her lose consciousness.

I've been administering this anesthesia for many deliveries here, just as I had at Robertsboro Hospital. Over time, I realize that the gas seems to work a lot better at Saint Jude's. Or maybe these patients are quieter and have less pain? Not likely.

Our anesthesia department has just acquired an oxygen analyzer. I use it to check the calibration of the delivery room machine. To my dismay I discover that the machine isn't giving 50 percent nitrous oxide, 50 percent oxygen as the dial states. It is actually giving 80 percent nitrous and 20 percent oxygen. This is unacceptable and dangerous.

I put a warning sign on the machine and run downstairs to alert the chief.

When I speak to Dr. Uberdo about it he's busy at his desk.

"It's all right, Emily." He wags his head. His pudgy cheeks and mouth screw up.

"That machine has been giving good anesthesia for years. It works fine."

"But, Doctor, it really isn't okay now. These mothers and babies need more than 20 percent oxygen. We're taking a chance that somebody could get hurt from this. We don't even know if we're affecting these little baby's brains. And the mothers are going under a lot deeper than is safe without airway protection."

"But, Emily," he whines, "it works fine! The obstetricians are happy. The patients are happy. And everything goes good. Leave it alone!"

I can't believe his attitude. I'm frustrated and angry. At home that evening, I go over it in my mind. Finally I decide what to do. I sit down at my typewriter and carefully compose a letter to the hospital administrator. I realize George Wasserman doesn't have much medical background, but I bet he'll understand the situation in dollars and cents.

The letter spells out how the hospital could possibly be sued if a brain-damaged child is born at Saint Jude's and the mother has been given anesthesia on this faulty machine.

Satisfied that I truly need to take this drastic action, the next morning I shove the letter under the administrator's door at 6:45 a.m., on my way to the OR.

Within hours, an obviously peeved Dr. Uberdo comes into the room where I'm giving anesthesia. He growls, "I'll take over here. You need to meet with Mr. Wasserman."

The balding administrator stands tall when I enter his office. He indicates a chair and we both take a seat. My letter lies in front of him in the center of the big mahogany desk. As I answer his questions, he grimaces. I explain in even more graphic detail the possible scenarios.

"I recommend that the machine be replaced immediately. We might be able to acquire a refurbished machine that is still under warranty. Whatever you decide, I feel the situation is urgent. And we are legally responsible for our anesthesia students, as well."

Two weeks later a new anesthesia machine is installed in the delivery room without fanfare. Success! But that night, at home in my bed, I have a shocking nightmare. I wake up in a cold sweat. In the dream it is nighttime. A knock comes at the door. I am alone. I open the door to find a policeman standing there.

"There's a very dangerous man in the neighborhood, ma'am. Whatever you do, don't open the door! For anyone!"

"Okay, Officer. Thanks for the warning!"

I close the door in my darkened foyer.

Then I see him.

He is already in, hiding behind the door.

My heart almost stops.

Waking in wide-eyed terror I sit up in bed.

What is that all about?

As I mull over the dream, something seems strangely familiar about the evil man behind the door.

Who does he remind me of? Dark skin, short, with a round face . . . Dr. Uberdo! Oh my gosh. This dream could be a warning. I just thought of him as ineffectual. But this dream is so powerful! What can it mean? Well, I certainly disregarded his wishes and went over his head when I wrote that letter to the administrator.

Over the next few weeks the dream is always in the back of my mind. I watch everything carefully. Dr. Uberdo seems to be his usual noncommunicative self. On the surface everything seems the same. Then little problems and coincidences begin to crop up. After a busy Tuesday evening I open the door to the dark on-call room. There is a putrid stench. When I investigate, it is coming from the adjoining bathroom. The toilet is blocked up with a large amount of reeking feces and filthy water overflowed onto the floor.

Next my little black book goes missing from my emergency box. This book is a collection of my personal notes about unusual surgeries, lists of drug combinations and other valuable reminders I collected over the course of my career. Somehow it mysteriously vanishes.

Dr. Uberdo cancels his lectures to the anesthesia students. This leaves the students in a quandary. The national certification exam they have to pass is extremely tough. A nurse anesthetist must successfully complete it before being employed. As their instructor I feel legally vulnerable with no anesthesia doctor involved in the school. I continue to work hard with my students, motivating them to study on their own as much as they can. They form a study group. They challenge each other with tough questions and theoretical situations, generating a lot of discussion and research.

A few weeks later I receive a call from Robertsboro Hospital with a good job offer. Now that Dr. Panute is gone, they want me back. It's a lot closer to home and I gladly accept. When I announce to Dr. Uberdo that I'm resigning he can barely veil his eagerness to be rid of me.

It's been a challenging three years for me at Saint Jude's. By now, several students have graduated, become certified and are providing anesthesia services as far away as Ghana, Hawaii and Texas. The current students are well on their way and I have confidence that with a little more hard work, they will succeed, thanks in part to the program I designed for the anesthesia school. I bid them farewell.

ANOTHER CLOSET

ROBERTSBORO HOSPITAL GIVES me a big welcome back. The OR staff is always looking for something to celebrate, but they act like this is extra special. The injustice of my being driven out by Dr. Panute was taken personally by the OR nurses and anesthetists. They were aware it could have happened to any one of them.

A new Chief of Anesthesia has been recruited from a big medical center, Dr. Hershey. My old friend and colleague Dr. Navana Misha introduces me to him. Apparently ever since Dr. Panute resigned, Navana has been working with the hospital administrator to have me reinstated.

With relief and gratefulness, I enter the OR my first day. No more teaching or testing. No big responsibility of keeping patients safe while anesthesia students are learning. Also, my best friend Michelle and I will be working at the same hospital again.

I deeply appreciate this anesthesia career. It is amazingly hard but has made me mentally and physically tough. I can sleep any-where, any time. I can be up all night and still be alert and function-ing, with the help of coffee, of course. I've learned how to size up patients in the ten minutes while they're conscious before I give them anesthesia. Sometimes they share things they've told no one else.

A young woman with belly pain was under anesthesia for exploratory surgery.

After a thorough abdominal exploration Dr. Alverez commented to the team, "I can't find anything wrong with this woman. Everything inside her is completely normal."

I spoke a little tentatively, "Do you believe in psychic pain, Doctor?"

"What do you mean, Emily?"

"Well, when I met this patient, her eyes were all red and her face was streaked with tears. She confided to me that her husband is being unfaithful to her. He's in love with another man. He doesn't know that she is aware of it. They have four kids and she has no employment skills or family to fall back on. She seemed to be grief-stricken and feeling hopeless."

"I guess that could make anyone sick. You might be onto something, Emily. How come she didn't tell me this?"

"I don't know, Doctor."

So yes, even though I sometimes can't stand my job, I'll never leave. There is a deep and mysterious connection between the anesthetist and the patient. We seem to actually enter the person's body and see what is happening. We sense things before they become a problem. Merge. That's what seems to happen. We merge with them and take care of them.

One afternoon fourteen-year-old Lydia doesn't come home from school. By suppertime I start calling around to her friends. No one knows where she is. Dusk is falling when I frantically notify the police. Finally the phone rings around midnight. She has been found at a shelter for runaways fifteen miles away. Lydia does not want to come home. After a lot of counseling and discussion, she admits herself into the adolescent unit of a local mental hospital. I'm her mother and I'm not even allowed to visit for the first week.

What has happened to my little girl? We didn't even have an argument. This is reminding me of what my mother went through years before, being away in a mental hospital for months, being subjected to electric shock treatments. I feel like my entire world is collapsing around me. I thought I was a good mother. Of course I get mad and yell sometimes, but what else can you do with teenagers?

When Michelle sees me at work she's surprised.

"What's wrong, girl? You look like you haven't slept in a week."

"Lydia ran away from home and now she's in a mental hospital." I can't keep my bottom lip from quivering.

"Hahaha!" Michelle chuckles. I whip around and snap, "What's so funny?"

Michelle hesitates. "Oh. Is she is doing it for a lark? Or is this really serious?"

That is a new perspective for me to think about.

Lydia is away for a few months, during which time she softens toward me. But even after she comes home, a wall is still there between us. I enroll her in a private school where she flourishes. They appreciate her artistic talents and encourage her to develop them. She becomes a prolific writer. By the time she's a senior, I at last believe I have Lydia figured out. One day I pick her up after school. After she is settled in the car I ask her, "We've had a brick wall separating us for a long time, Lydia. I wonder if it has anything to do with homosexuality." She inhales fast and her eyes cut over toward me for a second. Silence.

Then she whispers, "Yes."

I nod.

"Lydia, I love you. Whether you're gay or not you'll always have my love."

She breathes in deep and sinks back into the seat.

"Are you sure you know what you're saying, Mom?"

"Yes. And I really mean it." Inside I'm smiling. Finally the wall is gone.

How did I know how to handle this issue? Five intense years of spiritual work has opened my awareness of God's closeness. Before I talked with Lydia I asked for inner guidance. "How should I be? Should I be angry? Should I try to change Lydia into a straight person? Should I detach myself from her and not be involved? The answer comes miraculously through two close friends who, knowing nothing of my daughter's situation or my psychic question, share their own expanded understanding of homosexuality. Now I had the courage to ask my daughter, and also knew what my response would be. As the meditation master said: Just love her!

Several years later, I decide to tell Lydia what may have happened when she was conceived. Right before I became pregnant with her, I was taking the revolutionary new "Pill." When the drug first came on the market massive doses were being prescribed. I guess you could say that back in 1964 we women were guinea pigs. The manufacturer didn't really know what the correct dose should be. It had to prevent a pregnancy, but not be an overdose. Can you imagine the tiny fetus being bombarded with all that estrogen? No wonder Lydia has such a beautiful feminine body. But if the fetus is male, how would he develop? It could also explain her occult spina bifida birth defect that was first discovered when she was twenty one.

From babyhood my beautiful daughter hated wearing dresses. She never played with dolls the way little girls do. Her Barbie doll was subjected to rides in toy trucks and was bullied by GI Joe.

To be "out of the closet" is tremendously freeing for her. After high school graduation she pursues an RN degree at a prestigious university. For years she runs the medical floor at the same hospital where I got my nursing diploma.

THE  TOOTH

THE SCRUFFY MAN is having belly surgery, so I'll be intubating him. When I examine his mouth I note an upper front tooth is extremely loose, hanging by a thin piece of membrane. Dr. Navana is with me for the induction of anesthesia. Together we discuss with the fellow the dilemma of the dangling tooth.

"That wobbly tooth will most likely be falling out when we give you anesthesia, Mr. Williams, and we need to keep you safe. We must make sure it doesn't go down your throat and enter your lungs. As you can imagine, that would cause all kinds of trouble."

"No problem! Jest yank the ol' thing outta there. It's been botherin' me for ages." The man has no qualms about it.

"Fine, Mr. Williams. We're going to document that on our chart and get you to initial it, if you don't mind."

"Shore 'nuff. Let's get this over with." He signs the release form and we put him to sleep.

I always like to defer to the anesthesiologist in situations like this.

"Will you do the intubation, Navana?"

"Sure, Emily, and you just keep your eye on that tooth." She gently mask-breathes the patient while I sloppily lubricate the endotracheal tube.

"Oops! Sorry I got your arm all slimed with lubricant, Navana."

"It's okay. I'll let it slide." We chuckle behind our masks at our silliness.

We are unaware that the new Chief of Anesthesia has entered our operating room and is standing behind us. He has no knowledge of the prior tooth discussion or the man's signed release form. What he sees is this: As the anesthesiologist performs the intubation, the patient's big front tooth goes flying across the room and bounces on the floor. I loudly crow, "Wow! Look at that sucker go!"

The Chief's jaw drops. Suddenly we see him and the expression on his face. He must be thinking, "What kind of people do I have working under me, anyway?" He's probably envisioning a lawsuit and the patient's expensive dental work for which he will soon be paying.

We quickly bring him up to speed and show him the release form. When he sees that we're doing a good job he laughs out loud.

THE TUMOR

I SLIP UNNOTICED into the dark operating room. One big amphitheater light illumines the gruesome scene. The masked surgeon and his assistant are working on the man on the operating table. A watermelon-size tumor is being debulked from his right chest and armpit. His starkly pale skin contrasts with the deep crimson oozing surface of his chest and the black decimating lobules of the fetid tumor. His eyes are wide open and glistening. His teeth chattering. Each time the electric cautery tip sparks against his side, he twitches.

Waves of nausea and disbelief sweep over me. Why isn't he getting anesthesia? Has he refused it?

"You want me to give him something?" My voice croaks as I offer my services to the surgeon. I have no authorization to be there, let alone give anesthesia to this man I loved such a long time ago. I know I'm risking my license with that question. But I have to offer my help.

"No. We're finished."

A sickly helplessness overcomes me as I back out of that place. I retreat to the helter-skelter of the main OR where I can block it out of my mind, but not my soul.

It's been two years since Paul had the melanoma removed from his chest wall. After the surgery, he just couldn't stand the thought of having poison injected into his body so he refused chemotherapy. He went home with his woman to their hovel and tried some homeopathic heat treatments. During his occasional phone call I'd ask how he was doing, and the answer was always, "fine." Apparently he waited till the new tumor got too large to manage before coming back to Dr. Shillinger for help. He apparently refused anesthesia, so the bill wouldn't be so high.

Later I ask Dr. Shillinger what his chest scan shows. He tells me that Paul's lungs are full of tumors and that there is nothing else that medicine can do for him. The next day Paul asks me the same question. I pause, but I quickly decide he wants the truth. I say, "There are some nodules in your lungs, Paul." He goes silent and slumps back against the pillow.

Upset by his reaction, I retreat to the call room and phone Shillinger. He reassures me that I did exactly as he would have done if asked. Later that evening Paul wants to talk about it.

"When you told me I had cancer in my lungs, can you explain to me why I suddenly felt ecstatically peaceful? I don't understand it."

I have no answer, but I am relieved. He has protection. All is well.

Sweet Janice is by his side as he sits up in the hospital bed sipping diluted warm beer through a straw, celebrating the fulminating bloom of the melanoma. He's on oxygen. Every so often he leaps out of bed and cranks up the liter flow so he can breathe better. Never mind asking anyone to do it for him. I stop by when I'm on duty, but Janice never leaves his side. She spends the nights resting in a chair next to his bed.

When she leaves the room Paul asks me to read the prayer to him.

He knows Janice will cry if he asks her to do it.

No worry. I'm not going to cry.

I feel totally disconnected from him emotionally. After what he did to me and the kids, he can't upset me anymore. Softly I read the prayer to him.

The LORD *is* my shepherd; I shall not want. He makes me to lie down in green pastures; He leads me beside the still waters. He restores my soul; He leads me in the paths of righteousness for His name's sake. Yea, though I walk through the valley of the shadow of death, I will fear no evil; for You *are* with me; Your rod and Your staff, they comfort me. You prepare a table before me in the presence of my enemies; You anoint my head with oil; my cup runs over. Surely goodness and mercy shall follow me all the days of my life; And I will dwell in the house of the LORD forever.

(Psalms 23:1–6 NKJV)

Paul closes his eyes. His breathing eases. He is calm.

One day when we're alone he asks me, "How shall I die?"

My mind goes blank. Then from somewhere deep inside me these words flow, "Be gentle with yourself. You can just drift off to sleep, that way it will be easier on everyone else."

He nods silently.

One night a week later, Paul gently drifts off into his final sleep. Janice and our daughter Amanda, the only two people who have pure unadulterated love for him, are by his side. I'm in another part of the hospital giving anesthesia for the birth of a beautiful baby girl.

EMERGENCY

DR. BROMLEY IS one of the busiest surgeons at our hospital. A head and neck specialist, he operates on people with cancer of the mouth and throat. He's an elegant man who plays the cello, regularly performing with the community orchestra. He makes beautiful music at night and creates a blood bath in the OR during the day. Like most surgeons in the 1980s, he isn't skilled with cosmetic reconstruction. He'll chop out the diseased part and patch things up one way or another.

Doing anesthesia for these surgeries is upsetting. Even though he's removing their cancer, I find it difficult to watch the destruction of a person's face. Making post-op rounds, I have to steel myself before entering his patient's room. It's hard not to stare. I freeze my face to keep from involuntarily recoiling. Dr. Bromley cures their disease and saves their lives, but how can they face the world with only half a face? I wonder if the haunting music of his cello is actually a cosmic sound of lamentation, as an anguished universe cries out for these poor folks.

One night I get an emergency call to the room of Bromley's fresh post-op radical neck patient. "He's bleeding real bad!" The nurse sounds frantic.

I enter the hot room to face an alarming sight. The patient is sitting straight up in the bed. Two bloodshot eyes bulging with horror dominate the man's crimson face. Then I see it. From his neck a forceful stream of blood is arcing across the room, rhythmically pulsing one hundred and twenty times a minute.

Three nurses and a house physician stand aside, paralyzed. "Bromley's on his way in," the splattered doctor shouts, wringing his hands.

Carotid artery! I know what that means. He'll be dead in a few minutes. He's gasping for air. The man's panic stricken eyes plead with me.

"It's gonna be okay, buddy," I tell him as I step quickly to the bedside. I thrust my bare hand into the bloody neck wound. The heat and force of the hemorrhage guides me.

Got it! Suddenly the jet flow stops.

I snap, "Call Bromley again. I can't stand here holding this thing till it heals."

The man's eyes never leave my face. His rasping whisper begs, "Don't let go! Please!"

I stand there with my fingers pinching shut the hole in the carotid artery. I shift from one foot to the other. Time crawls. The fear-sweat and blood stench in the room almost make me swoon. Finally I sit down on the blood-soaked bed facing the man. His life depends on my tight fist in his neck.

Twenty minutes later Dr. Bromley bustles into the room.

"Get your hand out of there, Emily." He tries to wave me off.

I don't move. "Doc, get your gloves on. He's already lost a lot of blood. I'm not turning this geyser loose till you're ready."

A nurse steps forward and offers him sterile gloves and uncovers a tray of sterile instruments. I remove my cramped, aching fingers and quickly step back from the spitting gash. After a brief skirmish with the recalcitrant artery, the physician clamps and sutures the bleeder, stitches up the incision and matter-of-factly covers the man's glistening neck with a sterile bandage.

The patient's eyes still bulge with dread.

"It's all fixed now." I hope I sound reassuring as I pat the man's brawny hand.

In the adjoining bathroom I stand at the sink scrubbing my trembling hands for a long time. I murmur to the pale frown in the mirror, "I hate this job."

MERGING

WHY ARE MATT and I, a rather conventional almost middle-aged couple, not married yet? I continually ask God that question, but never get an answer. It seems strange to me but I am waiting until I know the time is right. We've been together almost ten years. One summer day we are visiting my parents at their beach cottage. Mom, Matt and I are sitting around the kitchen table as Dad enters the room. He is holding a large photo of his nemesis, my grandmother, who passed away several years ago. His eyes are red and his voice cracks as he speaks.

"I was so wrong about her, the way I judged her. I treated her so badly."

Dad's eyes begin to overflow. "If only I could have just one hour with her, I'd beg her to forgive me. I wish I could make it up to her."

I try to console him. "You can, Dad. Just talk to her now. Even though her body is gone her soul is still around. She'll hear you for sure."

Reflecting on my father's heart-softened outburst, I remember how he used to feel about my Gram's "living in sin" years ago. When my mother was a little girl, Gram divorced her physician husband. He was never seen or heard from again. None of us, his grandchildren, ever knew what became of him. Later in life, Gram had a companion who shared her home. He was the only "grandfather" we knew. My father did not think highly of his mother-in-law's relationship. Now for the past ten years Dad's dearest daughter Emily has repeated that history. He is very fond of Matt. I took care of both Dad and Matt when they had colon cancer. He knows how hard Matt works to care for me and my children. It seems something has shifted in Dad. Maybe he is reaching a deeper understanding of what's important in life.

Now we know. The time is right for a marriage celebration!

On January 8, 1983, amid our dearest family and friends, Matt and I have our special day. The sun is shining on a gloriously warm afternoon. Thanks to my brother Rich, we are surrounded by lush ferns and flowers in our newly remodeled sunroom. Mr. Boy, the old dog, inadvertently serves as bridesmaid and leads us down to the minister. It is a golden day.

Matt and I settle in and have many splendid times together. We add a pool to the backyard and spend leisure hours floating there with the sun sparkling on the clear water. We are surrounded by the fragrant garden we planted over the years. There are tomato plants and broccoli, cared for lovingly by Matt, and I have lots of roses, dahlias, black-eyed susans, and hydrangeas blooming all summer. We revel in our deepening bond.

I'm going to the ashram again. The old master passed away and now his translator has taken his place. Jason, who is now a monk, is urging me to meet her. Matt isn't interested. He'll gladly stay at home with the teens and the pool. We've given each other lots of freedom, right from the beginning. After all, why should couples have to do everything together?

The Appalachian Mountains are verdant. A July sun dapples through the leaves onto the blanket of emerald mosses underneath the trees. As I walk the wooded path that meanders along the water's edge, the lake is shimmering. For a long time I am mesmerized by the ripples in the water. Something deep inside me says, "At last. I understand." I don't know what it means, but I am aware of my profound tranquility.

As I hike, I think about the new meditation master who will be arriving in a few hours. These saints teach us to see God in everyone and everything. I try to immerse myself in that understanding as I roam the woods. All at once I notice a tiny mosquito landing on my forearm. "Oh, you must be the teacher welcoming me." I laugh as I swat my arm to squash it. With the intense OR environment I'm used to, I have no qualms terminating a mosquito.

The master arrives and gives a talk in the great hall. She talks about seeing God in everything. I'm sitting on the plush carpeting with several hundred other seekers, all of us listening with full attention. Then the master looks directly at me. She says, "And even when the mosquito bites you it is very sweet." She laughs.

"And if you're of a violent nature, you'll try to kill it!" She laughs again in delight, her rich deep laugh, and swats her arm right where the insect had been on my arm earlier that day!

How can she know that? How can this be happening? I melt into a slump of silent weeping. This is the same bottomless joy I felt when I met the old master. It is here again. I thought I lost it. But this time I know without a doubt that the source is not a nervous breakdown. Oh no. This is something profoundly uplifting.

Then I remember my other long ago vision, the brilliant loving column of light that embraced me that strange night in my meditation room. Could God really be everywhere and in everything?

Now her talk is over. People are getting in line to bow and express gratitude to the teacher. I slowly recover, and looking around, I notice several other reddened eyes. Nobody seems to notice me. Everyone is indrawn, as though approaching the sacred. Sweet music flows over the vast room as we move forward in our bare feet, slowly snaking ever closer to the master.

I stand before her. Our eyes meet. There is nothing but light. The place and people cease to exist. Time doesn't exist. I fall into her deep eyes. The light envelops both Master and Student as One.

Matt has been content to stay home while I visit the ashram, especially since I always bring him a fresh-baked loaf of their amazing bread. But now the loaves of bread aren't available for sale any more. Matt has been cooking rather bland vegetarian meals for us since he read Dr. Satillero's book, "Recalled from Life", in which the doctor describes his process of getting rid his own cancer. He thinks that maybe a visit to the ashram would help him learn how to season our food better. And also, there's that bread. We go together, and I sign us up for one of those two-day meditation events.

During that program, Matt is sitting in the back of the hall. In the dark, the meditation master walks around, up and down all the aisles. When she comes to him, she washes his bald head with rose water. He is stunned. At the lunch pause he can't even speak about it, but his head and shirt are still damp and fragrant. Later Matt describes to me the blazing, intelligent, loving light, the music, the power of God that he experienced. He is forever changed. He has become fearless. Even his death holds no concern. He feels he already knows God and will be happy to join that glorious realm whenever it's his time.

What a gift to me! My soul mate now understands my devotion to the Master and this spiritual path. He learns to play the mur-dung, an Indian drum; I play the harmonium. As we play and chant together our union becomes more joyous.

Early Wednesday Matt and I board the plane for Las Vegas. It is a pleasant five hours. We fly over the Grand Canyon and the snowy mountains of Aspen Colorado. When we land, the pilot wishes us good luck in "Lost Wages."

As soon as the plane door opens, I feel the difference in altitude, like I'm breathing the "smoke" from dry ice. After dragging our luggage all over the place to find our rental car, I have a heavy feeling in my chest and my muscles are weak. I take a couple of aspirin, in case I'm having a heart attack.

Matt drives us through the "Strip." What a place! Statue of Liberty, Eiffel Tower. Our hotel is luxurious and we even have a kitchenette. There is a deli/grocery store in the lobby. Soon I'm feeling better, and we set out to explore. The Venetian Hotel has a "town" on water with gondolas outside. Inside, Sistine Chapel paintings cover one massive ceiling. There is the whole main street of a town, with a fake blue sky—so real looking. I get a gelato in one of the little shops. There are musicians playing and all of a sudden a booming man's operatic voice joins them, singing the aria at full volume. A crowd gathers, swaying, and laughing when we realize the guy is a tourist just like us. When we shout "Encore!" his group says, "No, he has to leave or we'll miss our dinner!"

I got the concierge to get us tickets to Cirque du Soleil. It is an amazing experience with the music, costumes, and the strength of the performers.

Thursday we head for Sedona, a five hour drive through the deserts of Nevada and Arizona. We see the Hoover Dam. After that, very little traffic and no amenities for hours, just hills with little bunches of plants scattered on them, only what can survive. We see three hawks and look for bighorns, but no luck. The air is so dry our skin feels like sandpaper. I keep trying to breathe deeper. As we go further east, the desert changes again and yet again; grasses and yellow wild flowers, then blue-green little shrubs, then bigger evergreen shrubs. Finally as we get close to Flagstaff we are in pine woods, tall ones. The eighty-degree temperature has dropped to sixty-nine and breezy, cool in the shade.

We are able to bypass Flagstaff and go directly to Sedona. On the first twenty-five miles of Route 89A, towering red rock formations encircle us. I see the "sinking ship." Sedona is a quaint little town built to blend into the surrounding red rocks. At 12:30 we arrive at the Oaxaca Mexican Restaurant. A store next to it directs us to the second floor glassed-in dining room and gives us a 10 percent off ticket, too. We have the best chili rellenos ever! Everything is so good. We eat it all.

We check into the Days Inn, second floor, no elevator (my mistake), and head out for a few groceries. We are very attached to our yogurt and salad stuff. When we come out of the store the sun is setting. We make a mad dash to Red Loop Road, where the sun dramatically lights up the rock formations. We are alone. Majestic Silence.

When we get back to the room I break my sunglasses and we have to run out again to get some clip-ons for my regular glasses. I get some good ones. We settle in, have a toast with some good wine Matt found, eat a little salad and go to bed. Our jeep tour is at 8:00 a.m.

Friday: On the very bumpy jeep tour, we share the good front seat with an elderly cowboy driver. He shows us some usual landscape, a couple of interesting rock formations and plants. Then we check out and travel north through the incredible Oak Canyon. In Flagstaff we find the famous Black Bean Burrito & Salsa Company. We stuff ourselves with a fabulous tuna, rice and black bean burrito full of lots of other good things. A very busy place.

On the way from Flagstaff we see a mile-wide meteor crater. Desolate countryside, pure white grasses and dark green low shrubs. The land is for sale.

The Grand Canyon is truly grand! We drive to the east rim and climb the watch tower, about eight thousand feet above sea level. There are Indian drawings on the walls. With binoculars we watch the rafts coming down the Colorado River.

We check into El Tovar about 6:00 p.m. A guy is ranting about being a guest and not being able to park. We drive out to the lot and immediately find a good spot. A bellman carries our bags up the wide creaky staircase to our room. After we get gussied up a little, we go to the lounge, have wine, shrimp cocktail and bruschetta with artichoke. *So* good! The local kids are having high school graduation on the veranda so we sit inside the tinted picture window and watch unseen. Soon the sun is setting. We stroll around the rim and watch the purple take over. Black ravens and little sparrow-like birds fly around.

Oh, I forgot the most exciting thing that happened on our way to the hotel. An elk crossed the road in front of us. I jumped out and took photos. Another man was doing the same thing and we grinned at each other. I said, "We are lucky!" He said, "Yes, and there is another elk right over there." Sure enough, the second one wants to cross the street but several cars are stopped by now and she is scared off. She stands at the edge of the woods and poses for us.

Saturday we are up at 4:30, barely light out. We dress warm, in gloves and winter hats. It's about thirty-five degrees. As we approach, the silence is as immense as the canyon itself. We watch the peaks gradually come alive as the sun's rays angle ever steeper. Deer are feeding on El Tovar's front lawn. After breakfast we hike down the trail to Bright Angel Lodge, where the mules' smell precedes their appearance. Corralled in a stone circle, many mules of various colors stamp and move around. The Mule Master is instructing fifteen potential riders and warning them of the dangers. Off they go, down the side of the cliff—four hours down and four hours back in 120 degree canyon temperatures.

Later, around 4:00 p.m., we see them on the ascending trail, going slow and looking pretty bedraggled. At eight that morning a middle aged foursome had me take their picture prior to their hiking down to the very bottom. They planned to camp out there a couple of days, and then hike back up. Whew!

We meet a couple who shared where they saw condors last evening. We check out the Bright Angel Book Store and sure enough, in the back of the store is a door that opens onto a cliff ledge. Condors are flying around and perching on the craggy rock. They have recently been returned to nature after the remaining twenty-nine in existence were captured and coerced into laying lots of eggs. Now there are more than three hundred, some in Baja California and the rest here in the canyon. They have nests in caves and raise one young every two years. They mate for life.

Then I get my ice cream cone! A long line loops around in front of the concession. People are in line for fifteen minutes, but don't decide what they want until it's their turn and the server is standing waiting for them to make up their minds. Then, when they get to the end of the pay line, they don't even have their money out yet. Folks from other countries who don't know our currency are having trouble too. But the espresso chocolate chip is worth waiting for!

I pick out a beautiful turquoise necklace and earrings in the hotel shop as native singers and dancers perform for us.

Sunday we get a 5:00 a.m. wake-up call, jump in the car with hot cups of coffee and drive east to Lipan Point, the absolute best vantage point for sunrise. We are alone. We chant in this spiritual place.

Today we drive toward California, to visit my grandson, Jackson.

He is very excited to see us. It made me cry to hear his voice on the phone yesterday. All disappointment of not seeing Andrew was washed away.

We stop for lunch in Kingman and again, Matt materializes a fabulous Mexican restaurant. The whole town is having Sunday lunch there. We get enough food to feed four people for fifteen dollars. Heading west, we get to Barstow at 5:00 p.m. The California desert isn't as pretty as Arizona, just dry dirt, windy and hot. Must be over one hundred degrees. The Ramada Inn is nice but train tracks out back make me wonder what tonight will be like.

Monday: Trains went by all night long, but slow and quiet. We are up at six and drive through southern California's soft suede, rolling hills. Around Bakersfield we pass a whole forest of gigantic spinning windmills.

After we arrive at our destination, Jackson drives up in his gray Toyota pickup, with 183,000 miles on it. His face looks a lot like Andrew and me, sparkling blue eyes, long blondish curls, broad shoulders. He talks fast. We hug and I feel very close to my grandson.

After our time with Jackson, we hit the road again on our final leg home. After six hours of driving, we take a bathroom break at an old truck stop on the outskirts of Barstow. No gas or shade, we sit in the 120 degree car with all the doors open and grab a quick snack, then hurry on toward Las Vegas. Twenty minutes up the highway we realize we forgot to get gas in town. We have a quarter-tank left and we're in the desert. Eventually we come to a little gas station charging six dollars a gallon. Oh well, we gotta have it.

In Vegas we visit Mandalay Bay's Shark Aquarium. The lobby is large as an airport. We walk what seems like a couple miles, past windows framing skimpily-clad crowds around many sunny pools. The aquarium is spectacular. We are surrounded by sharks, on all sides and overhead.

Next morning we return the rental car, traverse the slot machine-filled airport and fly home. The home-going crowd is much more subdued. On our flight to Las Vegas, a woman sitting behind us kept laughing for hours. Also, Matt got in trouble with the flight attendant when he started exercising on the curtain rod separating us from first class.

As we get close to home, a wonderful wild lightning and thunder downpour welcomes us. My heart is full of love. Love is all there is.

BIG BLUE

I'M ON CALL for the next twenty-four hours, and it doesn't look good.

We've been operating for nine hours and the OR is still jumping. There is an emergency craniotomy scheduled. After being at the ashram all weekend I just want to sit still and meditate. But it is not to be. I set up for the "crani," and fortunately, the patient is in pretty good shape. The surgery proceeds uneventfully. As soon as I deliver the head-bandaged fellow to the recovery room the anesthesiologist I'm on call with delivers the bad news. The next case will be another craniotomy. It is very unusual for us to have two brain surgeries in a row. Robertsboro is a little community hospital. We ordinarily might have one craniotomy a month.

The second head case is underway and going well. We should be done in about two hours, I think. But I want to meditate. I feel very frustrated not to be able to be still and alone in a dark room. Then the most bizarre thing happens. A third emergency craniotomy is scheduled. At this news, I start to laugh. How weird can tonight get? Silently I say, "Okay, God, I finally get it! I don't need to meditate. I just need to be completely focused at what I'm doing and to totally enjoy it. I need to be in the moment and immerse myself in what is happening right here, right now. Boy, you sure have a tough way of communicating with me. I guess with a thick head like mine you need to be persistent until I get the message. Speaking of thick heads, are these craniotomies symbolic of you cracking open my head and pouring yourself in?" A smile creeps over my face. I better keep these ideas to myself or somebody'll think I've gone off the deep end.

Sometime after 3:00 a.m., the last patient is turned over to the recovery room staff and I clean up my OR. My work is finally finished. I schlep up the stairs to the on-call room. At last, I sit cross-legged on the bed for meditation. The room is dark. My mind is completely still. I close my eyes.

Immediately something extraordinary happens. Behind my closed eyelids a big blue ball of energy appears. Surprised, my eyes pop open, and there it is. Standing before me in the shadowy room is a gigantic scintillating ball about six feet high. It seems totally alive. The apparition is steaming with millions of cobalt, azure, cerulean and sapphire sparks, all whirling and shooting from within the mass. The range of bluish colors is phenomenal, more than I could have ever imagined. As I watch awestruck, the energetic atoms slowly disperse throughout the room and become the bed, the chair and everything including me. I am actually seeing how the material world is structured with these enthralling vibrant particles. I've read that scientists have proven this, but amazingly, I'm actually seeing it! Dare I say that I am seeing God?

Then the room becomes dark again. I lie down and drop into a deep sleep.

This night changes me forever. A living, intelligent blue energy within me is forming the world outside of me. I can never forget it. I see it happening all the time on the dark road when I'm driving at night. I see the blue Presence in sandy footprints on the beach and snowy shadows in winter. I rest in the blue ocean of the Great One of All.

CLICK

MY CAR CRUISES along, my headlights the only illumination along the deserted highway. It's been another long night on call. My lungs inhale the winter air deeply, a welcome relief after hours of breathing traces of anesthetic gases and various human stenches. I shrug my fatigued shoulders, reminding them to relax.

Suddenly, brilliant flashing lights and a loud siren shatter the serenity of the predawn. A police car roars up behind me. Oh no, just what I need right now. I pull off the road and wait. The noise abates, but the relentless strobe light reminds me of my booming headache. Gravel crunching under foot, a burly officer approaches my open window.

"Where ya' goin' in such a big hurry, Sweetie?"

His man-smell and cigarette breath repel me. I cringe deeper into the plush upholstery.

"I'm an anesthetist. I just left Robertsboro Hospital. I've been on duty all night."

"Yeah, right. You tryin' to tell me yer some kinda doctor or sumptin'? Lemme see yer license, hon."

I shove the card into his massive hand.

"Emily, huh? Li'l Emmy! Well, you're a cute li'l redhead ain't cha! How 'bout hoppin' in the back o' my squad car for a quickie before it gets light out? For the benefit of Law and Order, if ya' know what I mean. That way we can just forget about the ole speeding ticket. C'mon, whadaya say, Emmy-Girl?"

"Just give me the damn ticket, OFFICER!"

I glare at his badge. Officer James Shaeffer.

Rebuffed, he steps back from my car. Whipping out his pad, he scribbles fast, tears off the top sheet and tosses it in my face.

"Here's yer damn ticket, Bitch!"

He stomps back to his squad car, jumps in and guns it past me, spraying gravel against my fender and windshield.

Rivulets of sweat feel cold down my sides. My heart thumps a little slower now, but I oscillate back and forth between rage and terror. I slowly drive toward home.

Two weeks later:

"I got terrible pain in the belly, Doc. And I been throwin' up every time I try to eat somethin'."

"Well Jim, it looks like that old hernia of yours finally got strangled. You know I warned you in the past to get it repaired. Now we've got a real emergency on our hands."

"Okay, okay, Doc. Let's get it over with. I'm sick as a dog."

"I'll call the OR and get you scheduled."

The big policeman is propped up on the stretcher, his dark hair covered with a paper OR cap. An intravenous line drips into his arm vein at a lively pace. His beefy face looks pale and almost gaunt. Sunken into dehydrated sockets, his eyes nervously dart around the Operating Room. He takes in the cold green tile walls, the domed spotlights overhead and the blue-draped table laden with ominous stainless steel instruments.

A tall woman in green scrubs and cap approaches the stretcher. "James Shaeffer?"

"Yes, ma'am."

"OFFICER James Shaeffer?"

He looks closer at her unsmiling face and the lock of red hair escaping from her cap.

His eyes widen.

"Emily." He whispers.

"Yes, Officer Shaeffer. I'm your anesthetist. First, we need to put a naso-gastric tube down your throat before you get the anesthesia. It goes in your nose and down into your stomach. It'll be a little unpleasant, but it's for your safety. We need to make sure your stomach is empty. Vomit entering your lungs can be deadly. We're going to take good care of you."

Officer James Shaeffer cringes deeper into the mattress.

Under the sheet, his hands involuntarily move to protect his private parts.

THE VISION

I SIT IN meditation with several hundred other devotees. We're attending another two day ashram event. The Guru is in her chair down in the front of the hall. The soft drone of the tamboura seems to deepen the stillness. My mind is completely quiet, which is unusual for me, quiet but alert. Suddenly I am experiencing an inner vision. In my mind's eye a big white tractor-trailer truck comes rolling along. There is a blue V design on the front of the truck. I am in a vehicle that is stopped way up ahead of the truck. I am aware that the driver of the truck does not realize that my stalled vehicle is directly in his path. I mentally shout to him.

"STOP! STOP!"

But he doesn't hear. The truck is coming very fast.

Instantly I know. "Oh! It is my TIME."

I whoosh out of my body the instant before the crash.

Then the meditation is over. Everyone gets up and slowly leaves the hall.

I ponder my meditation experience. I know I just experienced my death. Amazingly, I feel no fear. I think, what a great way to go. No sickness or getting old and feeble. The only part that bothers me is, what about my family? Will they have to see my body all messed up?

For the next three days at the ashram, everywhere I go there is a foul smell.

Wow, somebody must have some rotting sore on her body or something.

This is very unusual. Devotees are always taking showers and it's rare that anyone would have an unpleasant odor. But it seems to be everywhere I go.

Finally, on the third night a special ceremony is held in the temple. The women, all bathed and dressed in saris file into the room. The saint's statue sits cross legged before us, draped in an ornate cape. His pedestal is steeped with bouquets of roses, gardenias and other fragrant blooms. There are gigantic bowls of fruit, nuts and loaves of yeasty breads placed around the altar. A hint of sandalwood incense is in the air. Each one of us holds a tray with a lit candle as we chant sacred Sanskrit mantras.

The smell is here! I can't believe it. In this sacred place, abruptly my mind opens fully and I get it. This is the smell of death. Death is stalking me. I better pay attention to that vision. Death can come at any time. After I have this understanding, the smell disappears.

When I go home I get all my affairs in order. I pay off my bills and create a notebook so Matt can deal with things after my death. I don't talk about the vision. But the question remains. What about my family? Will they have to see my body all messed up?

A few days later I'm working late at the hospital. The Emergency room calls Code 99. When I arrive on the scene, I'm told that the woman's car stalled in the fast lane and a tractor-trailer struck her from behind. Our team tries to resuscitate her but her neck is broken. Nothing can be done to bring her back. She is dead. AND THERE ISN'T A MARK ON HER BODY.

Humh. My question has been answered. Thank you, God.

THE ROSE

THE ORTHOPEDIC ROOM is in full swing. The anesthetized patient is already strapped onto the fracture table, a torture-like apparatus that supports her body while the broken hip hangs suspended in air. The wiry surgeon sways from side to side as he soaps up the injured area with dripping sponges. Pop music is blasting from the radio.

"Hey!" he yells to the circulating nurse. "Turn it up! Turn it up louder!" Ol' Dr. Rimple is in a nasty mood today.

When she turns up his music, I nonchalantly reach up and adjust the volume on my monitor so I can hear the patient's heartbeat.

"Hey! Put it louder! I can't hear it, now she turned that damn monitor up!"

The circulating nurse glances sideways toward me as she increases the racket from the radio.

Again I adjust the patient's monitor up another notch louder.

"You bitch!" SLOP! A big wet sponge smacks against the heart monitor, slides down and lands on to the machine, ruining my anesthesia record. I reach for the phone.

Softly, "Get Dr. Greenberg in here right away!"

The anesthesiologist is used to Rimple's tirades. He appears at my side almost instantly. We huddle together behind the anesthesia machine and I whisper, "Maybe it might be better if some other anesthetist takes care of this patient. I don't think my being in this room is a good idea, Doctor."

Looking sheepishly relieved that this might be a simple solution, the man takes over and I slip out the door.

This feud has been going on between Dr. Rimple and me for a while now. I don't know how it started, maybe something Rimple's scrub nurse might have said. Babs has a knack for getting him riled up. The problem is, I'm on call till eleven tonight.

As luck would have it, at 9:00 p.m. Rimple has another surgery. He despises me so much that he doesn't speak to me through the whole operation. I'm at the head of the OR table where all the controls are, but when he needs the table position changed he has the circulating nurse relay the message rather than ask me directly. He never makes eye contact with me. I keep my focus on the patient but the tension in the OR is tight. The distressed circulating nurse goes out into the hallway and vomits up her dinner. At this time of night there is no one else who can take over for me, but somehow we get through it. By 11:10 the patient is awake and doing well in the recovery room, and I am finally off duty.

I go out to my car in the doctors' parking lot. I like to park there when I work late because it has better lighting than the nurses' lot. It is a steamy night, still about eighty degrees. No one else is around. Only two more cars are still parked.

I have an eerie feeling that something's not right. As I approach my car I smell something. A stink seems to be coming from the front of my white Mercury. In the gloom I can't see anything unusual. I lean over the hood. The distinctive reek of fresh urine radiates from the air conditioning vent in front of my windshield.

Oh my gosh! Somebody just urinated on my car. Who would do this! It's very fresh.

At that moment I hear a motor gunning away in the dark.

Dr. Rimple left just a few minutes before me. A spine-chilling feeling comes over me. If he would do this, what else might he do?

The ashram is my haven from all the madness of the hospital. All this weekend there is a chant going on in the open-air pavilion. It is a tranquil setting in the woods with a mountain stream gurgling gently nearby. Birds darting among the tall pine trees seem to join the chant with their chirps. Many devotees stay for hours, chanting and swaying in the sweet current of musical vibrations, while a constant trickle of others slowly enter or leave. Sitting there cross legged, I become totally absorbed in the chant. I drown in the splendor of my silent inner Self as I sing with my whole being.

The question doesn't arise for several hours. In the beginning I would never have asked it. But as my immersion in the harmony deepens, something softens inside me and the question does come up.

I know there isn't, but Dear God, is there possibly anything I could do to stop the hostility with Dr. Rimple?

Swiftly the answer comes. In my inner vision I see myself standing before Dr. Rimple. I'm smiling and then I hand him a rose.

My eyes pop open.

NO! NO, NO, NO!

God! No! I would NEVER give that reptile a rose! Never!

But there it is. My ecstatic feeling is gone.

Sunday evening I head back home. On the way, I stop at a garden store. My brother asked me to get him a plant for his room. The philodendrons are lush and I choose one that will do well in his sunny ashram space. Next to that plant is a vase of long-stemmed roses. They are pale yellow but the tips of the petals are red.

Well, if I WERE to give that jerk a rose, this would be the perfect one. It looks like it's been dipped in blood. I buy one.

Monday morning I feel numb. I lay the rose on the passenger seat as I drive to the hospital. But I'm NOT giving it to anybody.

When I arrive in the department, there he is, walking just ahead of me in the hallway.

I catch up to Dr. Rimple. He glances at me warily. Calmly I bow my head and offer him the peace rose.

"I wish we could work together in harmony, Doctor." The words ascend from an unforeseen place inside me. I look up and see that he looks stunned.

"Thank you. Thank you. Thank you." That is all he can say. His eyes glisten. He puts his arm around my shoulders and together we enter the operating suite.

Later that day a recovery room nurse approaches me.

"I heard what you said to Dr. Rimple this morning. It was extraordinary, and it got me thinking. I've been estranged from my son for over twenty years. Now I see that I can try something to change things between us. Thank you. I understand how hard that must have been."

This is a moment of change. Dr. Rimple still has his temper tantrums, but no matter what, he and I always treat each other with respect. And my ego has crumbled a little.

THE POWER

SRI RUDRAM IS a chant that I love. This Sanskrit prayer is originally from the ancient scripture Krishna Yajur Veda. I appreciate its universal approach to God. It describes the entire universe as His form. And it is He who appears as all these beings, sentient and non-sentient, positive and negative. The melody is only four notes. Often I sing the Rudram in English.

"Salutations to Lord Shiva, the primordial Guru, whose form is existence, consciousness and bliss; who is transcendent, calm, free from all support, and luminous."

Now every morning before work I sit cross-legged on the floor in my small meditation room and am transported to an inner world of joy and freedom.

"Salutations to You who are the oldest and the youngest. Salutations to You who exist in roaring waves and in still waters."

One day I'm assigned to work with old Dr. Bering. His woman patient has a terribly painful infected left breast. Three months ago he operated on that very breast, removing a benign cyst.

"She's sound asleep, Doctor," I give him a nod that he can make his incision.

He slices open the oozing abscess. Behind my mask my nose scrunches up. He reaches into the wound and quickly pulls a large putrid sponge out of her breast.

My eyes widen.

Oh my gosh! He left that rag inside her boob three months ago!

The surgeon doesn't say a word. He just sews the breast back together, bandages her up and stalks out of the room.

The very moment that I arrive at the recovery room with the patient, Dr. Bering charges in, shouting loudly at the groggy woman.

"It's all your fault, you stupid woman! This infection was caused by you not taking care of your diabetes! You must have let your sugar levels get sky high for this infection to happen!"

My mouth drops open. The truth of what really happened is horrible enough. Why does he have to make the woman suffer psychologically by falsely accusing her of doing something wrong? It was his damn mistake. This guy may have been a good surgeon in the past, but I think he's blind as a bat now. I'll bet he ran in here and started hollering at her just to make sure I'd keep my mouth shut!

A few days later I attend the monthly anesthesia meeting. The whole team is in attendance. When the opportunity arises, I bring up the Dr. Bering situation.

I speak out, "This week Dr. Bering pulled an old sponge from a woman's breast and blamed the patient for the infection. He can't see well enough to be operating on people. What can be done?"

I am hoping my colleagues will agree. Maybe the department will stop providing anesthesia service to him. He has to be stopped.

There is dead silence.

I speak again. "Could we all just refuse to give anesthesia for him?"

My comment is ignored and the meeting soon adjourns. When everyone leaves the room, Dr. Hershey, the Chief, speaks to me privately.

"Everybody knows about him but there's nothing we can do. He covers his traces very well. Even the hospital board knows about him. I'm sorry, Emily. I know how you feel."

Next day, during my 5:00 a.m. meditation, I ask Lord Rudra for help.

Okay, Rudra. I did everything I know to stop this man from hurting patients. Now the job is up to you. I begin to chant the sacred verses. And when I sing the verse that says, "I will put all those who treat us as enemies and those whom we treat as enemies into your open mouth," I stop and mentally place Dr. Bering into Rudra's mouth. The next morning I do the same thing. On the third day, as I chant that verse, a gruesome sight flickers for just an instant in my mind. I catch a glimpse of an ugly dog-like creature eating the doctor up.

When I get to work that day I am assigned in the C-section room. While setting up, word comes that Dr. Bering has just been found dead in bed.

I hold onto the OR table to keep from falling down. How could this have happened? Dead! He is dead!

Rudra!

In a state of shock I somehow get through the day. Fortunately I have the next day off. Again I sit in my special room to chant. But first I speak sharply to Lord Rudra.

"Good grief! I didn't mean for you to bump him off! I just wanted you to stop him from hurting people!"

Suddenly there is a tremendous explosion outside. Throwing open the front door, I run up the street toward the smoke. A navy jet plane has crash-landed two blocks away. There is a lump in my throat. I am awestruck.

Surprisingly no one was hurt. The jet basically double-parked on a little side street. In order to avoid crashing into the houses, the heroic pilot steered it down till two hundred feet off the ground before he ejected. That should have killed him. Miraculously he got hung up in a tree and had only minor scrapes and bumps.

"RUDRA! OKAY! You have shown me your omniscient power! I don't think I'll be putting anyone else into your open mouth. I promise to treat you with more respect. Honest!"

So maybe this is all a big coincidence. Perhaps my ego is saying I have a God who will help me in a hopeless situation. I don't know. You decide for yourself.

A MIRACLE

TO ENHANCE MY practice of anesthesia, I'm taking a neurolinguistic programming course. I go every weekend for nine months. The course is amazing. It demonstrates how much we can change our reactions to our thoughts, feelings and the actions of others. For me, it is a wonderful course in learning how to create our future reality, by consciously changing our thoughts. We learn how to help our client switch from one perception to another in a painful situation.

I use this technique on a sixteen-year-old patient having emergency surgery after shattering the bones in both his legs. Since he is too unstable for anesthesia, during the procedure I sit at his head and speak softly to him. I have him "sit in the balcony" above us and watch the surgery from afar. I wasn't sure what would happen, but he is able to do this easily, with no discomfort. The surgeon uses a local for the skin and muscle, but can't numb the bones as he pierces them with metal pins and places traction on them. The young man is peaceful and pain-free and the surgeon is amazed.

Over the months of working together and practicing neurolinguistic programming on each other, the class members get pretty friendly. Some of them share that they walked on burning coals after a four-hour session with a motivational speaker who uses this technique. I am dubious that my tricky mind could ever be convinced to do that without getting burned.

I come up with something else almost as dramatic.

136

I plan to walk on water. That's going to be my thing.

When the course ends, I invite everyone to my home for a picnic to celebrate graduation. As the high point of the party, I try to walk on the water of my swimming pool. Even after a few drinks and several attempts, it is not happening. Even with my flippers on, I take two or three running steps across the pool and sink, sink, and sink.

A few weeks later at the ashram I am outside the temple. It is ten o'clock at night. I stand there for an hour every evening. My assignment is to nicely inform devotees that the temple is closed and direct them to the meditation cave. My last night here is the eve of a big holiday and many preparations are going on around the temple. The fountains in the upper garden are tested. While I watch, the sprinkler system drenches the newly laid lawn of grass sod.

Long after dark, folks are still working under spotlights in the distant rock garden, planting and weeding. Leaving my post, I decide to walk across the vast lawn to see their progress. Halfway across I realize that the lush turf is totally saturated.

Uh oh, there go my new sandals. I didn't plan to get them wet. Oh well. It's done now.

I continue through the sogginess, enchanted by the intricacy of the spotlighted rock garden flowers and sedum. Droplets on every blade of grass are sparkling like jewels.

Then I quickly walk to my car in the back parking lot. Why aren't my feet feeling cold? Here in the mountains the temperature has dropped to about forty-five degrees. My socks and sandals had sloshed through all that waterlogged grass. I sit in the driver's seat and reach down to feel my feet. Completely dry! My breath sucks in deep. There is no sign of wetness on my socks or sandals!

What? How could this be? I walked across seventy-five feet of thick, dripping, wet grass, and not a drop touched any part of my shoes or socks.

The realization comes.

Oh I get it, God. I walked on water! Not in the spectacular way Jesus did it. But I just walked on water and did not get wet. Oh, how

You love to grant even my silliest desire. Such a great and hilarious God You are!

At next morning's breakfast my brother reports, "The Master just spoke and told me that my sister is becoming very beautiful, but I am going bald because I think too much." I chuckle at how much my brother hates the thought of going bald. But for her to say that I am becoming beautiful? Why would she say that? The Master knows something has happened to me. Not just "walking on water." Everything feels different today. I see sparkling blue particles everywhere I look.

I leave the ashram and drive the four-hour trip home. It takes five hours. I am so rapturous that I miss a couple exits, but it doesn't even matter.

Arriving home, I am alone. The day is glorious. I vacuum the pool, put on my swimsuit and slip into the velvet water. I am the water. I am the sun playing on the bottom of the pool, swirling in mystical patterns of fire. I dive into the flames of love. Yes, love is what it is. Love of what? Nothing. And Everything. I dance around and around in the pool, the silken waves of water and bliss twirling and blending into ONE. Round and round until I feel I might actually lose consciousness. I better get out of the pool now.

A crow in the neighbor's tree squawks, "Congratulations! Congratulations!"

Matt arrives home from work. When I hear his car pull into the driveway I wonder, will I be able to see God in him too? With open arms he walks around the pool to me and with the Master's words he says:

"…I welcome you with all my heart." His words make me cry. We embrace for a long time. My soggy bathing suit soaks his suit and tie.

We go to our favorite Italian restaurant for dinner. Even though we are eating our salads, the waitresses keep bringing other patron's salads to our table. And we laugh. The laughter is a great release for all that joy in me. Expanding delight bubbles up from my deepest Self.

That night I sleep soundly. Upon waking I find the top sheet has been twirled and twisted into an amazing spiral in the middle of the bed. Maybe I've been dancing all night long. Inside me I keep hearing Shankaracharya's eighth century prayer over and over:

> You are my Self. You are my Reason. My body is Your Temple. My five breaths are Your attendants. All the pleasures of my senses are objects to use for Your worship. My sleep is Your state of Samadhi. Wherever I walk, I'm walking around You. Everything I say is in praise of You. Everything I do is in devotion to You, O benevolent Lord.

LET ME CALL YOU SWEETHEART

HE'S LYING ON his side, covered by the white sheet. I stand beside the stretcher for a few minutes, then tentatively ask, "Hello . . . Hello?" My patient is scheduled for a hernia repair, but this isn't what I expected to see. Penny, the preop nurse hands me the chart.

"He's micro cephalic and has cerebral palsy too. He hasn't moved a muscle since he got here ten minutes ago. I guess he's hiding from us."

I have to give this guy anesthesia in a couple minutes and need to get some kind of rapport. I touch what looks like a shoulder under the sheet. The white mound on the stretcher quickly jerks away from my hand and begins trembling.

"Wow! You really are scared, aren't you?" I pick up the corner of the sheet and come face-to-face with a red-faced little man whose deeply sunken eyes are scrunched tight. Still trembling, his fists jerk the sheet back up again, but not fast enough. My olfactory receptors catch the acrid smell of his fear. I move to the desk to review the patient's paperwork.

"Oh, he's blind, too! Great! No wonder he can't figure out what's going on. I hate to just manhandle the poor guy. But he won't even let me touch his shoulder!"

"Yeah, they had a heck of a time getting his IV started, but it's running well now."

I position myself at the head of the stretcher. "Well let's get this show on the road! Will you help me wheel him around to Room Two?"

Penny hesitates. "First let's try a heated blanket on him."

"Good idea." When the nurse places the warm cover over him the trembling human mound seems to shrink up even smaller.

"Oh, Benny, poor little Benny, don't be afraid! It's okay. Everything is really okay! I'm not gonna let anybody hurt you, little guy!" My sing-songing to the mentally challenged fellow doesn't get the result I want either. Faint guttural moans come from under the covers.

We push the stretcher into the fluorescent glare of Operating Room Two. The surgeon is still out scrubbing up. His radio is playing one of those dreadful oldies he subjects us to when he's working. "Let Me Call You Sweetheart! I'm in Love with You" softly emanates throughout the green-tiled OR. Ordinarily I'd just tune it out, but now I'm desperate.

"Craig, would you mind cranking that boom box up all the way? This is a good one!" Over his mask, Craig's eyebrows move up almost into his hairline. He knows how I feel about these rustic tunes. He shrugs and turns the volume way up.

I sing out, full and deep, even louder than the radio.

"LET ME CALL YOU SWEETHEART! I'M IN LOVE WITH YOOOOOUUU!"

At that, scrub nurse Darlene starts chuckling behind her mask, her eyes all crinkly at the corners. She can't resist. She joins in, tentatively at first, then belting it out with gusto right along with me. Now even Craig's deep bass resonates, "I'M IN LOVE WITH YOU!" As the three of us croon, we grab the bottom sheet and gently lift Benny from the stretcher onto the operating room table.

His trembling has stopped. "LET ME CALL YOU SWEETHEART! I'M IN LOVE WITH YOOOOUU!" echoes and reverberates against the tile walls of the OR.

As I get ready to administer the anesthesia, Benny begins moaning again. This time it sounds different. He's right on pitch! And his deformed little hand begins tapping up and down in time with the music.

Then Benny smiles! The three of us look at each other and hoot with delight.

Even after Benny is asleep, "Let Me Call You Sweetheart!" continues running through our heads. Craig and Darlene hum at times. I join in softly when I'm not too focused on vital signs.

The surgeon doesn't get it. "I thought you guys didn't like my music."

"This is a pretty darn good one," I respond.

Over her mask, Darlene's sparkling eyes smile at me. "Yep."

FORGIVENESS IN 1984

I'VE BEEN VISITING the meditation ashram for a week. One night my roommate Sally and I share our divorce stories with each other. I end up telling her all the gory details about how thirteen years ago, Paul abandoned me and our three little children, moved to another state to avoid child support, and lived a life of freedom, building small sailboats. Eleven years later, he died of malignant melanoma at the age of forty-four.

After Sally and I finally settle down and say good night, I lie wide awake. I'm vibrating with energy. Look at the state I've gotten myself into just thinking about that despicable man. He's been dead for two years and I still abhor him.

Moonlight shines in the open window and a cool breeze encourages me to take deep breaths to calm myself. As my mind quiets I feel something pop inside the center of my head, sort of like a small firecracker going off. There's no sense of discomfort. I just notice it and wonder what has happened.

Then my story begins to replay itself with a whole new perspective. I see the bitchy dependent housewife I was during our marriage. Up to now, I have never taken any responsibility for the failure of our union.

Then suddenly I realize that when Paul did those mean things, a hidden strength inside me began to expand. I was forced to take on challenges that I always believed were far beyond my ability. Because of him I am now a respected anesthetist employed at a respected hospital. I've been able to keep my children in our little home and care for them well. And for the first time I'm learning how to truly love.

I begin to understand that his actions helped to set me free from the terrible box of limitation I was stuck in.

Lying there, I my heart begins to flood with gratitude to Paul. He dedicated his whole lifetime to me. He behaved worse and worse, first not holding a job, then becoming physically abusive to me. The final blow was the "other woman." I believed marriage should be forever, but that was more than I could live with. When he died years later, his father and sister hated him. Two of his three children refused to accept him. What a hard role it was for him to play. But who knows how many lifetimes I would have remained stuck. I needed somebody to do this for me. And he did it so effectively. It really worked. I have become a Joyous Being. Thank you, Paul! Thank you, thank you, THANK YOU!

Later I learn what the little firecracker going off in my head that evening is all about. Through the practice of meditation, a chakra in the head opens, bringing deeper understanding.

THE FAST LANE

IT'S A RAINY night. Streetlights flash by as the ambulance screams toward Robertsboro Hospital. They are hunched over in the back, vigorously administering CPR. Upon arrival they quickly wheel the patient's stretcher into the emergency room. The EMT is sweating as he holds the mask on the woman's gray face and squeezes the Ambu bag.

He calls out, "Her car stalled in the fast lane. Hit by a tractor trailer from behind at forty-five miles an hour. He was tryin' ta stop, but didn't see her car in time. Plus the wet road didn't help. We got our lines wide open but never got a pressure. Heart rate is weak."

The doctor yells, "Let's get 'er intubated and see what we got." Protecting the patient's neck, he inserts the endotracheal tube and secures it. She is ventilated with 100 percent oxygen. A nurse relieves the EMT guy and takes over manual chest compressions, her breath coming in short bursts each time she presses on the patient's chest.

Somebody notices the lady's red hair.

"She looks familiar. Anybody know who this is?"

"Remember that anesthetist who worked here? She was real good at intubating people. If I'm recalling correctly, isn't her name Emily?"

"Oh yeah, Emily! Wow! Bad luck for her tonight. Who would'a thought we'd ever be resuscitating her. This is her game!"

They do everything they can but nothing could bring her back. Broken neck and there's not a mark on her.

Later the ambulance crew is standing out back having a smoke. The rain has finally stopped. The radio in their vehicle is softly chanting, "Lady in Red, I'll never forget the way you look tonight."

"What a night. Weird accident, huh?"

"Yeah. And didn't it sort of look like she was smiling?"

"It did. Weird."

"Wake up, Emily! Your procedure is over. You're in the recovery room now. Everything went perfectly. Your gall bladder is out and you are doing great."

"Oh my gosh! What a nightmare I just had! Am I really alive? Oh yeah, I feel the pain coming on. I'm definitely alive. Thanks for taking good care of me. Great anesthesia. I'm awake!"

AFTERWORD

These diary entries, while fiction, have been
influenced by real happenings.
May Emily's story be a tribute to all the brave and silent nurse
anesthetists, those unsung heroes, the "watchers," who have
been keeping us safe and pain-free in ORs, delivery rooms,
and surgical centers all around the world since 1932.

None of us knows what our "grand finale" will be. What really
matters is that each moment is a pure treasure complete in itself
yet adding to the prior one until the pattern is complete.
I used to think that writing down all these adventures might
change my thinking somehow at the end. But the truth is, in the
process of "waking up," each of our experiences builds on the last,
creating change within us so gradually that we hardly even notice.
The perfect reality is to love it all—the good, the bad,
the beautiful, the ugly, the funny, the weird.
To have nothing to gain, nothing to lose.
To just BE.

ABOUT THE AUTHOR

MARY ELLEN ADMINISTERED anesthesia in various hospitals and surgery centers for over thirty-four years. During this time, the practice of anesthesia and surgery advanced tremendously, becoming gentler and less invasive with each new development.

The 1970-80's timeframe of this novel was before there were scavengers on anesthesia machines, or Schrader valves to prevent the mix up of oxygen and nitrous oxide lines, before arthroscopic, laparoscopic procedures. These diary entries give us a chance to vicariously experience some of the difficulties dealt with by health care workers.

Mary Ellen also creates digital photographic art. Her work is published regularly in a local publication. She illustrated The Elsinore Tree, a children's book about Hamlet. She sings barbershop harmony in a chorus and meditates daily. In her dreams she still administers anesthesia and these dreams often act as catalyst for her stories. Mary Ellen's sailing excursions with her brother Tony will influence her next novel.

She lives in Lansdale PA with her husband Lee.

CPSIA information can be obtained
at www.ICGtesting.com
Printed in the USA
BVOW08s1824050218
507266BV00001B/30/P